Earl of Renshaw

A Sweet Inspirational Regency Romance

For the Love of an Earl, Book Four

COLLETTE CAMERON

Blue Rose Romance®

Sweet-to-Spicy Timeless Romance®

Other Collette Cameron Books

For the Love of an Earl
Earl of Wainthorpe
Earl of Scarborough
Earl of Keyworth
Earl of Renshaw

Check out Collette's Other Series
Castle Brides
Heart of a Scot
Seductive Scoundrels
The Culpepper Misses
The Honorable Rogues®
Chronicles of the Westbrook Brides
Highland Heather Romancing a Scot
Daughters of Desire (Scandalous Ladies)

Dedication

An Irish blessing for Maya—
the sweetest Irish lass—and my faithful readers too.

May love and laughter light your days and
warm your hearth and home.

A very stormy April afternoon

St. James Street, London, England

Braced against the blustery spring wind determined to finagle a way inside his black-caped greatcoat or sweep his hat from his head, Sanford Brockman, Earl of Renshaw and future Marquess of Trentholm, lifted his chin and glowered at the dismal charcoal sky.

Unlike the unfortunate souls he usually turned his infamous glare upon, causing them to quake in their shoes, the heavens did not care that they'd earned his infamous and formidable disfavor.

With the vengeance of a scorned lover, the tempest had come upon the city unexpectantly. Pouting pewter clouds poured forth every drop of precipitation they contained in an unyielding sheet of bone-chilling, soaking rain.

The petulant day matched his grave mood.

Hours before, Sanford had attended his sister's wedding, where he'd had to endure not only the beaming bride and groom and his blissfully married younger brothers' smug expressions but the annoyingly frequent question from other guests: when was *he* going to find himself a bride?

Not any time soon, by thunder.

Why was everyone so blasted eager to see him dragged to the parson and leg-shackled?

In eerie confirmation, a jagged streak of orange and blue lightning lit the ominous firmament as angry thunder crackled and grumbled in the distance.

At the resonating boom, a woman scurrying past squeaked in alarm and, with a worried glance over her shoulder, ducked her head and quickened her already frantic pace.

Sanford had become so perturbed by the guests' repeated prying into his private life that he'd indulged in a moment of imprudent flippancy and said, "I assure you, when my betrothal occurs, it shall not be fodder for the gossip rags or newssheets."

Yes, he well knew his duty, not only to the earldom but to the marquisate. An heir, a spare, and perhaps, as Father had done, a third son to ensure the continuation of the line.

In his four-and-thirty years, Sanford had not met a woman he would consider taking to wife. Regardless, whoever the future Countess of Renshaw was, her lineage would be impeccable, and she would possess decorum, deportment, and a mild, biddable temperament. Should she be winsome, attractive, gifted with musical talent, fond of horses and dogs, and a tolerable chess player, so much the better.

Theirs would be a comfortable arranged marriage based on commonalities and no unrealistic expectations.

Today, when Lady Pandora Osborne—meddling matchmaker extraordinaire—had turned her gimlet eye upon him with a distinct, contemplative, and wholly unnerving glint, Sanford had deemed it time to remove himself from the festivities posthaste.

Straight from his sister's wedding breakfast, he'd sought a much-needed reprieve from the merrymakers at White's. A glass of fine scotch had done much to warm his belly and mellow his peevish disposition.

Weddings were supposed to be a time of rejoicing and celebration, and yet he always found them tedious and exasperating in the extreme. All of that unbridled emotion, unrestrained giddiness, sycophantic posturing… *Nauseating*.

He was hard put to prevent a shudder and his upper lip from curling in disdain.

A once glossy but now mud-splattered ebony coach trundled past, the lobster-red wheels and horses' hooves churning the murky water flooding the cobbled lane and accumulating in narrow streams along the edges.

Filthy spray shot sideways. On the opposite side of the street, a gentleman shook his fist and cursed as he leaped out of the way and turned his back. A smattering of dirty water splattered the vaguely familiar man's side, but he'd pulled his hat low on his forehead, and his long cloak made it impossible to identify him. Another chap joined him—a servant of some sort, given his rough clothing—and they put their heads together in earnest conversation.

Not the best location for a serious discussion, particularly if they did not want another coach to drench them. They peered up and down the street before parting in opposite directions.

It seemed Sanford was not the only fellow stupid enough to take a walk in the worst gale of the year. However, he wasn't as imprudent as three of his four younger brothers and sisters. Every one of Sanford's married siblings had lost their bloody minds and married for love.

Buffleheaded idiots, all.

Marissa had not Come Out yet, so a chance remained she would make a wise match, unlike the others. He held his brothers and sisters in great affection, but, in truth, he did not understand them any more than they understood him.

Neither was he the least motivated to remedy that disparity.

Indulging in a rare parting from dignified behavior, Sanford snorted aloud, earning a curious glance and a toothy grin from a thin lad running by in an ill-fitting gray tweed coat.

Love.

That mystical, farcical, trumped-up, nonsensical emotion caused people to flout responsibility, obligation, and duty. To disregard life-long expectations, strictures, and even honor.

Ronan had married a governess emersed in scandal. Benjamin eloped with an actress—or had Isadora been an opera singer? It should've come as no surprise that his impetuous, unladylike, and wholly unconventional sister, Corinna, would choose as her husband a blackguard like Baron Strathmore, rumored to have set the fire that killed his entire family so he'd inherit the barony.

It did not matter that Strathmore had been completely vindicated.

He'd been tainted by disgrace. His reputation smudged beyond repair. Scandal left a stench in its wake that one could never be rid of, and that was why Sanford avoided any association with ignominy.

Stifling an oath, he clapped his hand to his head to prevent the wind from absconding with his beaver hat. Marching along, he held the hat in place and cursed the weather. He should not have sent the coach ahead to The Wicked Earls' Club to await him, but he'd needed the exercise.

Physical exertion always calmed him and helped to clear his thoughts.

In recent years, fewer nobles joined the earls' secret society, and several former members had married and left the club. With increased newspaper circulation, keeping the earls' personal affairs private had become nearly impossible. He wouldn't be surprised if the club closed its doors in the next decade.

An unforeseen pang of remorse stung him at the thought. The earls' comradery was not easily replaced.

Heads bent against the relentless wind and rain, a pair of women wearing thin shawls huddled beneath a tattered umbrella as they scooted along the buildings, using the structures as a partial buffer against the torrential onslaught.

Sanford stepped aside to avoid having his eye poked out by the umbrella. His foot sank into a deep puddle, the contents of which consisted of a repulsive mess of rain, manure, and other undefinable muck.

Fiend seize it!

Scowling, he shook his leg, glowering at the revolting residue clinging to the once-shiny shoe. He should've changed into his boots before leaving Pelandale House earlier. Mouth pressed into a grim line to stubble the curse rising to his tongue, he increased his pace.

His stocking squished in his shoe.

Squelch. Squelch.

This confounded day just kept getting worse and worse.

Perhaps Sanford would skip The Wicked Earls' Club and spend the afternoon and evening at his cottage, Hydeaway House, instead. From time to time, he chose to stay there, relishing the peace and quiet. Something hard to come by at Father's mansion, where Sanford normally resided.

That was his one concession to selfishness. All else in his life was geared toward the earldom, to preserving its dignity and honor.

Sanford originally bought the quaint cottage to install a mistress in. Except no woman intrigued him enough to make that life-altering commitment. The place had become a sort of private sanctuary. He did not even permit his valet, Brewster, to accompany him, and thanks to the caretakers, Mr. and Mrs. Goggin, the house was always ready for him to pop in without notice.

A slow smile curved his lips.

Yes, that was what he would do.

That would also save him the inevitable gushing conversation about the wedding that was certain to take place at home. Of more importance, he would be spared his father's and stepmother's ever more frequent suggestions of a suitable bride.

Feeling much improved with his decision, Sanford turned the corner.

Ah, there was his coach.

Walton, the coachman, had likely taken refuge in The Wicked Earls' Club kitchen, where he typically enjoyed a hot cup of coffee, a tasty snack, and flirted shamelessly with the maids and cook.

The rain had abated to a drizzle—at least temporarily—as Sanford approached the club, and a few intrepid souls ventured outside. Coach and horse traffic increased as those eager to return home scurried forth before another shower deluged the city.

The dark clouds and the onset of late afternoon cast the street in a multitude of grayish shadows.

That same angry gentleman he had seen earlier gestured wildly at a trio of men forming a semi-circle around him. They all shook their heads and, appearing perturbed, peered up and down the street.

Sanford crumpled his forehead in concentration. He felt certain he must know the chap, but the fellow's name escaped him. Ah, well. It was of no consequence.

Anticipating a hot bath, a simple dinner, one of Mrs. Groggin's scrumptious desserts, and reading before a roaring fire as he sipped a superior cognac, Sanford rapped on The Wicked Earls' Club door.

The panel swung open, revealing a tall, liveried footman.

"Good evening, Lord Renshaw."

"Please inform my coachman that I have changed my mind about this evening." Sanford jutted his chin toward the vehicle. "I shall await him in the coach."

"Very good, my lord."

Sanford turned away before the door closed and returned the nod of a gentleman with a lady on his arm.

He opened the coach and had raised a foot to climb aboard when he froze.

What the bloody…?

Someone cowered inside on the floor.

2

Five terrifying heartbeats later…
Inside a stranger's luxurious coach

S oaked to the skin and shaking so hard from bone-chilling cold and mind-numbing fear that her teeth chattered, Grace Dooley tried to curl into an invisible ball on the coach floor.

Go away.

Eyes squeezed shut, she prayed the stern-featured stranger she had glimpsed before ducking her head and pressing her face into her knees would leave.

Please leave.

Shut the door.

I just need five more minutes.

She needed a little more time to catch her breath and partially restore her equanimity before resuming her frantic flight. However, providence was not feeling benevolent. In truth, providence had not been kind or benevolent to Grace for over two months.

Nine weeks of hellish existence since her employer's fleshy son had returned after traveling abroad for three years. Six and sixty days of dashing into alcoves, putting a bracing chair beneath her chamber door handle, carrying a letter opener in her pocket, and fending off his inappropriate advances.

"Who are you?" the man snapped. "Why are you in my coach?"

The deep, grating voice seethed with annoyance and impatience.

Blast, he'd draw attention, and that was the last thing she wanted.

Jerking her head up, Grace's gaze collided with mahogany eyes, fringed with ridiculously thick eyelashes beneath severe raven eyebrows. Everything about this man fairly screamed power, privilege, and unyielding will.

She shoved several strands of sodden hair off her face with one hand while raising a forefinger to her freezing lips and sinking to her knees.

"Shh."

Dread clawing her spine, Grace searched past his broad shoulders for a terrifyingly familiar face.

"I should think it obvious." Even to a simpleton, which this gentleman clearly was not. "I am hiding."

She swung her gaze back to his.

"*Hide-ing?*" he pronounced the word slowly, dragging it out several syllables as if trying to discern the truth. Or perhaps he thought Grace was queer in the attic.

"Please, my lord."

Surely a man dressed as finely as he and who owned such a grand coach was a peer. Even if he was not, Grace had learned men adored flattery.

"I beg you, do not give me away." She clutched her hands to her chest where her heart beat like a bird caught in a fowler's snare. "I shall leave in a couple of minutes. I swear."

Great shudders vibrated through her, and she wrapped her hands, stiff from cold, around her shoulders in a vain attempt to warm herself. Swaying, she closed her eyes, lightheaded from hunger and her petrifying flight with nothing but a small bag of her earnings and personal effects tied at her waist and hidden beneath her pilfered apron.

Lord above, she'd never been this wretched and cold in her entire life.

She had escaped the house cloakless and wearing a maid's uniform that she had managed to hide piece by piece. It had taken her a fortnight to gather each article to avoid raising suspicion among the staff and her invalid employer's dissolute son. It had been a blessed miracle that a chambermaid had left last month, putting the household another maid short and providing an unassigned uniform.

The reluctance of young, attractive females to work at Gibson House of late could be attributed directly to Hollace Wyndam.

Reprobate, degenerate, bounder.

His gaze probing, the lord's high forehead creased into a stern three-lined frown before he veered his keen attention to his right and then his left.

"Why are you hiding?"

Every clipped syllable dripped with suspicion and perhaps accusation too.

Of course, he doubted her. He probably believed Grace had committed a crime.

Who wouldn't?

Even she recognized how guilty she appeared crouched in the coach. Could she be charged with trespassing for stowing away in the empty vehicle?

Theft for the garments she wore?

Grace bit her lower lip, misgiving churning her empty belly.

How much should she tell him?

More on point, could he be trusted?

Hollace Wyndam might well be an acquaintance of his.

"I am waiting." Annoyance fairly crackled around him.

The thunder had sent Grace bolting into the unattended carriage. For as long as she could remember, thunder and lightning had terrified her.

Everything about this gentleman, from his narrowed, flinty eyes, chiseled jaw, and wall-like shoulders and chest, suggested he lacked compassion and mercy. He brushed long fingers across that sculpted jaw, the movement jerky with impatience.

"I suppose you are trying to concoct a believable excuse for stowing away in my coach."

Grace stiffened her back and tipped up her chin, inexplicably angry with him.

No, not just him.

She was furious with all men of privilege who used their position and exerted their power over women to bend them to their will. Men like Hollace Wyndam, who believed he could crook his fat finger, and she would fall into his bed. And when she resisted, he'd threatened to lock her in her chamber.

That was when she realized she must escape him and hoped her friend, Joy Morrisette, and her doctor husband would temporarily take Grace in until she could find another position. But in her flight, she'd become lost, and the hackney driver she tried to hire took one glance at her rumpled maid's uniform and sneered before moving on to another fare.

"I am running away from my employer's son. I

have been her companion for nearly a year, but since his return from touring the continent, he's been determined to force me to become his mistress."

She would never be any man's mistress. *Never.*

Not only because she had been raised to be a woman of moral character by Mrs. Hester Shepherd, the proprietress of Haven House and Academy for the Enrichment of Young Women, a foundling home and school, but also because such an arrangement would destroy Grace, wearing away at the core of her integrity and self-worth.

She shoved a sodden strand of hair off her cheek, then yanked her soaked cap firmer onto her head. "I even fabricated a faux fiancé to dissuade him, to no avail."

Make of that what you will, you pompous, judgmental boor.

The lean contours of his lordship's face grew impossibly severer.

Because he did not believe her…or because he did?

He removed his hat and skimmed a black leather gloved hand over jet-black hair, shoving it off his forehead as he heaved a great sigh.

"What am I to do with you?" he muttered, clearly inconvenienced and unconvinced.

Granite glittered in his eyes.

His regard unflinching and wholly unnerving, he replaced his hat.

Was he too much of a gentleman to toss Grace out on her bum, or was he considering calling a constable?

Still on her knees, she hobbled forward. Willing her shivering to cease so she might speak clearly, she managed through chattering teeth, "Nothing, my lord. You needn't do anything. I shall be on my way."

Before he pressed charges.

Contempt etched his ruggedly handsome countenance, and again she was not certain if he directed his scorn toward her or the unnamed man who had sent her on this perilous flight.

It mattered not whether he believed Grace or not. Her gut told her that he wouldn't help her. Men of his ilk were all the same. Too toplofty, arrogant, and full of their own self-importance to deign to assist someone beneath their illustrious station.

She was not surprised.

Nevertheless, disappointment still sluiced through her.

The best she could hope for was that he would not have her arrested.

"I shall go right now."

And pray no more thunder rattled the heavens.

Bracing her hand on the plush claret-colored velvet seat, Grace clutched her saturated bag and, poised at the opening, poked her head out.

"There you are!"

Oh, God.

"No." A terrified half-moan, half-gasp escaped her.

Grace shrank back into the coach's dimness.

Wyndam had found her.

Such potent dismay and fright engulfed Grace that she nearly swooned. Instead, she glared daggers at the shadowy form blocking the opening.

This was his fault.

If the big, brooding brute had not been determined to interrogate her, she might've escaped Wyndam's clutches.

She raised what surely must be terror-filled eyes to his lordship's.

Nothing shifted in his gaze or expression to indicate he empathized with her plight.

Wyndam trotted up to the coach. In truth, his approach consisted of an arduous, uneven gait.

Breathing heavily—the man was at least two stone overweight—he twisted his thin lips into a sly smile. Gasping, he fished a rumpled, soiled handkerchief from his pocket beneath his cloak, then mopped his sweaty forehead.

"I say, Renshaw, old chap," he wheezed between great panting puffs. "Pray tell me, why is my"—he eyed Grace's bedraggled and sopping uniform— "*maid* inside your coach?"

Ah, so Wyndam did know this Renshaw fellow.

"I am *not* your maid, Mr. Wyndam," Grace snapped, beyond caring about courtesy. "I am—*was*— your mother's companion."

Was until this morning.

Grace hopped down, bumping into Renshaw and forcing him to take a step backward. Not before she caught a whiff of manly cologne. Sandalwood and cedar?

Wyndam generally reeked of sweat, and his fetid breath could curl the bark off trees.

A pair of women had stopped, expressions rapt, to watch the exchange, as well as a tall, handsome chap who appeared to be a coachman, and three expensively attired gentlemen preparing to enter the building before which the coach was parked.

A nice little crowd to witness her disgrace.

Grace had already peeved Renshaw. She might as well thoroughly provoke the man and pray he possessed a shred of decency beneath his greatcoat.

She pasted a brilliant smile upon her lips and linked her arm through the crook of Renshaw's elbow. A wave of dizziness assailed her, but she locked her knees and blinked away the inky spots swimming before her eyes.

A tremor rippled up her spine and spread across her shoulders.

He shot her a questioning glance.

Mouth and throat oddly dry, she swallowed.

It hurt bloody awful.

Perfectly lovely.

The last thing Grace needed was to fall ill. At least not until she reached the Morissettes'. Brandon Morrisette was a doctor.

Mayhap Renshaw could be persuaded to take her to their house.

Not likely, however.

Not after she'd made a spectacle of him, even though it had been unintentional.

Renshaw's eyebrows shot to his impressive hairline, but before he could speak, she leaned into his side in what she hoped was an adoring manner. After all, she had no experience flirting or pretending to be enamored.

"Not that it is any of your business, Mr. Wyndam, but I am meeting with my betrothed."

3

*B*etrothed?

If Sanford had not had decades of controlling his reactions, his jaw would've hit the ground with a loud thud and perhaps bounced a time or two. Instead, he schooled his features and adopted a benign mien.

Was the chit utterly mad?

Had she escaped Bedlam?

No, Wyndam said she was his housemaid.

Though they did not travel in the same social circles, he'd met Wyndam previously once or twice.

He had been out of the country for some time, hadn't he?

Given the rotting sod's reputation, Sanford did not

blame the girl for hightailing it. It did not take a genius to guess why she had fled her employer *if* she really did work for Wyndam's mother.

Gazing down at her upturned oval face and almond-shaped eyes such a dark blue that they competed with the deepest ocean, something unfamiliar twinged behind Sanford's breastbone. Curious, this sudden proclivity to protect her.

Having escaped the ill-fitting mobcap balanced haphazardly upon her head, several strands of hair as black and shiny as a raven's wing dangled around her slender shoulders. Bright spots of color glowed on her ashen face, and her eyes had taken on a glassy, unfocused appearance. She trembled, though whether from cold, fear, sickness, or all three, he could not discern.

Her eyes, framed by sooty lashes, silently begged for his help.

Sliding Wyndam a cautious sideways glance, she licked her lower lip, desperation fairly radiating off her.

Releasing a caustic laugh, Wyndam shook his head.

"Come, Miss Dooley. You will have to do better

than that. Anyone who knows the Earl of Renshaw knows he would never—*never*—lower himself to wed a common chit so far beneath him. His tastes are much more refined, and his standards far, far loftier."

"You presume to speak on my behalf, Wyndam?"

Arctic air was tropical compared to Sanford's tone.

Wyndam shuffled his feet but did not apologize for overstepping. "I have wasted the better part of a day searching for you, gel. It is time to return home."

Who pursued a runaway maid, anyway? Unless she'd committed a crime.

Sanford examined Miss Dooley from beneath half-closed eyes.

Had she?

Many a pretty face concealed a wicked heart.

Wyndam reached for her arm, and she cringed, pressing into Sanford's side.

"No." A tremor shook her raspy voice. She coughed, an ugly rattling behind her ribs that betrayed her brave demeanor. She shook her head, the ugly, ill-fitting cap sliding farther to the side. "I shall not go with you."

"You will be dismissed if you do not." Wyndam's features hardened into condescending haughtiness.

Bloody idiot.

It was as obvious as the rather astounding pimple on his nose that Miss Dooley had already quit her position. Not a light decision for a woman in service.

Again, that ferocious, foreign need to protect her rose up within Sanford.

He, who had always scorned masculine displays of aggressiveness and prowess.

Wyndam terrified her, and Sanford needn't be a seer to understand why. He would wager his earldom that what Wyndam planned for Miss Dooley did not include dusting, cleaning fireplaces, polishing silver, or making beds, though a bed would likely be involved.

Miss Dooley's inky eyelashes fluttered as she swayed against Sanford.

The girl was on the verge of collapse, despite her bravado.

He instinctively snaked his arm around her narrow waist, steadying her and holding her upright.

Devil take it.

What a bloody, rotted conundrum.

As a gentleman, common decency demanded Sanford assist the girl, but her colossal, very public lie about being his betrothed tempted him to turn his back and leave her to deal with Wyndam alone.

She had put him in a deuced, discomfiting position, and Sanford detested being manipulated. He loathed being the object of speculation and rumors even more, which is why he'd spent a lifetime avoiding any hint of ignominy.

Now, within a span of a few minutes, a mere nymph of a girl had managed to place him in an impossible situation.

A snide, superior smile skewed Wyndam's mouth as he cradled his weak chin between his thumb and forefinger. He believed he had her trapped.

In point of fact, he did.

Rain began pelting them again, yet none of the bystanders scampered inside.

After all, how often did a person get to witness such a provoking scene?

"Your affianced is remarkably silent, Miss

Dooley," Wyndam slid his gaze to the rapt onlookers.

A third woman had joined the other two, and they dipped their bonneted heads together to whisper behind their hands. None seemed the least affected by the rain. It proved quite remarkable what unpleasantness and inconvenience one would suffer for a succulent morsel of gossip.

Miss Dooley stiffened her shoulders and pulled herself erect.

Despite his anger and frustration, Sanford could not help but admire her fortitude. She had taken a gamble and lost, yet she did not wilt or dissolve into tears.

Head held high, she swept her indigo gaze over the assembled gawkers.

The earls standing at the entrance to The Wicked Earls' Club exchanged speaking glances, then entered the club. Their discretion could be relied upon.

However, a swift scan of the remaining bystanders confirmed Sanford's worst suspicion. They eagerly regarded the exchange, and no matter the outcome, this debacle would make titillating conversation in the upper salons in short order.

Miss Dooley met Sanford's gaze, an apology in hers. Defeat lingered there as well. And hopelessness.

A fragile, nascent smile curved her poppy-red lips.

Too red.

She was ill.

Only an idiot could miss the signs.

And still, Sanford could not summon the words he knew she desperately needed him to say. To keep her safe. To keep her out of Wyndam's clutches.

She stepped away, her movement stilted and uneven as she lifted a slender, pale hand to her forehead.

Primal satisfaction etched Wyndam's features as a predatory gleam glittered in his eyes.

The bounder thought he had triumphed.

Hadn't he?

No, by Zeus. He had not.

Sanford grasped Miss Dooley's elbow. "Come, let's enter the coach. The rain increases."

She turned toward him, dazed and confused. "I…"

"Just a bloody minute." Wyndam stomped forward a step. "If she leaves with you, I shall have her charged with theft within the hour."

She blanched, teetering, and Sanford felt certain he was the only thing keeping her on her feet.

Rage contorting his features, Wyndam pointed at the bedraggled gown and apron she wore. "That attire is not hers."

Excited whispers from the onlookers met his declaration.

Sanford arched an eyebrow in the superior fashion he'd mastered and which cowed most men.

"And what other clothing would a maid wear, Wyndam?"

Barely refraining from curling his lip in scorn, Sanford raked his gaze over the man, finding nothing to redeem the churl.

"Yes, but the uniforms do not belong to the staff," Wyndam blustered, just short of a sniveling whine.

Pinchpenny.

"I shall personally see that the uniform is returned to you, so there is no need to contact a magistrate, is there?" Sanford held the other man's gaze until Wyndam shifted his sideways.

"No." Wyndam pinched his mouth into a

disgruntled pout resembling a goose's hind end. "But I expect them by week's end."

"My lord…?" Miss Dooley's voice had diminished to a gossamer thread.

Sanford glanced down an instant before her eyes rolled back into her head, and she fainted dead away.

Swearing under his breath, he caught her and lifted her into his embrace.

Every instinct told him he would regret what he was about to do.

Blister it; he already did.

With a nod to Walton, he climbed into the coach and gently laid Miss Dooley on the seat. He arranged her as comfortably as he could, noting the shallow rise and fall of her chest.

She needed a physician.

"Where to, my lord?" Walton asked, his expression carefully neutral.

"Hydeaway House." So named for the refuge the cottage had come to be. In truth, there was nowhere else to take this mystery woman.

The door clicked closed with a portentous snick,

cloaking the interior in muted half-light.

As Sanford settled onto the other seat, the coach lurched forward. Chin on his fist, he regarded the minx who'd just upturned his well-ordered life.

"What havoc have you brought upon me, Miss no-given-name Dooley?"

4

Hydeaway House, London
Early the next morning

The sounds of someone puttering around the fireplace hearth stirred Grace from a deep slumber. Eyes closed, she put a hand to her aching head and turned over in bed.

Wait.

Where were the hard lumps?

She patted the plush mattress, and her eyes flew open.

Fern-green velvet met her shocked gaze as she stared upward.

Green?

No. That was not right.

The walls of her bedchamber at Gibson House were

painted a faded, pale yellow.

Her former bedchamber, that was.

She no longer worked for Mrs. Wyndam.

Grace lurched upright and simultaneously gasped as pain stabbed her skull and every joint in her body screamed in protest at the abrupt movement.

Where was she?

How had she come to be here?

A cough rattled her ribs.

When was the last time she had been this sick?

Glancing down, Grace crumpled her forehead.

She still wore the maid's uniform, absent the apron, and someone had removed her mobcap and unpinned her hair, allowing it to tumble about her shoulders.

"Dearie, lie down." A stout woman, worry creasing her kindly, round face, bustled toward the bed. Cheeks apple-red, she brushed her hands on a ruffled white apron covering a rather startling floral puce gown.

She passed Grace a handkerchief. "You mustn't overdo."

She placed the back of her hand upon Grace's forehead and made a *tsking* sound. The aromas of violets and starch wafted from her.

"You have a fever, miss."

Through her befuddlement, Grace peered at her, trying to place the kind stranger.

She had no more idea who the servant was than she knew where she was.

"Where am I?"

She winced as the words emerged in a hoarse, scratchy rasp.

Rather than answer, the woman fluffed the pillows encased in lavender-scented cases, then urged Grace back until she partially reclined upon them. She then poured a glass of water.

"I'll wager you are thirsty."

Grace was. Terribly.

She accepted the water. The cool liquid soothed her fiery throat, and she drained the glass, then passed it back.

"Thank you."

"I am Mrs. Goggin."

The woman dampened a cloth in a nearby basin and, after wringing it out and folding it into a neat rectangle, laid it on Grace's forehead before tidying the bedding.

It felt blessedly cool on her hot skin, and she closed her gritty eyes.

"I shall let his lordship know you have awakened, miss."

"His lordship?" Grace whispered, forcing her heavy eyelids open.

"Yes, indeed." Mrs. Goggin nodded, her chins folding and unfolding like a fleshly fan. Pride shone in her toast-brown eyes. "Sanford Brockman, Earl of Renshaw. Future Marquess of Trentholm."

An earl.

Grace's rescuer was a confounded earl.

No, a future marquess.

Just her rotten luck.

Memories of yesterday came flooding back, swamping her senses.

The dim coach.

The wet and cold.

Hollace Wyndam chasing her.

Renshaw's cologne. The curious crowd. Her

paralyzing fear.

And Lord Renshaw's uncompromising visage…

Fingering the coverlet's silk edge, Grace asked, "Did his lordship bring me here?"

He must have done, of course.

Only, where *was* here?

Hands braced on her ample hips, Mrs. Goggin gave a proud nod. "Indeed, he did."

Wonder of wonders.

Lord Renshaw was not an unfeeling, cold-hearted cad, after all.

"So worried was he about you that his lordship even had Dr. Pritchard pay a call last evening to make sure you were not on death's door. Doctor will be 'round this afternoon to check on your recovery."

Mayhap not death's door but hovering about in the foyer, for certain.

A citrine-eyed white and black short-haired cat sporting a neat feline mustache leaped onto the bed.

"Ralph, you naughty scoundrel," Mrs. Goggin scolded, leaning down to remove him, but Grace shook her head.

"Leave him, please. I like cats. I like all animals, in truth. Except for snakes, but they are reptiles, not animals."

Grace had always wanted a pet, but circumstances hadn't given her the opportunity. Good fortune hadn't exactly fallen into her lap, beginning with being abandoned as a child.

Extending her hand, she permitted the cat to sniff her fingertips.

"Hello, Ralph."

Ralph pranced forward, purring loudly, and, with the superior air only cats are capable of, allowed her to rub behind his one black and one white ear.

"You have made a conquest. I always say cats know good people," Mrs. Goggin said approvingly. "I shall fetch his lordship and a wee bit of breakfast for you too, Miss…?"

She gazed at Grace expectantly, her hint as broad as her backside.

"Oh. I am Grace Dooley."

Grace bent her mouth into a weak smile.

"Thank you, Mrs. Goggin. You have been most

kind. I am sorry to inconvenience you."

Another cough shook Grace's shoulders, making her lungs burn.

"Pshaw, it is no inconvenience. 'Tis nice to have another body around. As busy as his lordship is, his visits are infrequent."

Mrs. Goggin pursed her lips as if realizing she had revealed too much.

"I am truly grateful," Grace said to fill the awkward silence.

"I shall be back in two shakes of a lamb's tail." With another warm smile, Mrs. Goggin departed the bedchamber.

Ralph curled up on Grace's lap and proceeded to fall asleep, his nose tucked beneath his paws.

Idly petting the cat, she stared at the pleated canopy.

Yesterday, she'd fled Gibson House, afraid for her honor, and today, she awoke in an earl's home. Forehead furrowed, she glanced around the bedchamber. Though tastefully decorated with fine furnishing, this bedchamber lacked the ostentatious silk wallpaper, crown moldings, and plasterwork common in *haute ton* homes.

What, exactly, was this house used for?

Grace was not positive she wanted to know.

She had no sooner finished the thought when a sharp rap echoed outside the open door, drawing her attention across the chamber.

The doorjamb framed Lord Renshaw, reminiscent of yesterday when his broad shoulders had blocked the coach's opening. He strode farther into the room, causing the small chamber to shrink considerably with his rugged, masculine presence.

Attired in black except for his shirt, cravat, and unadorned charcoal-gray waistcoat, he exuded the same measured reserve she had sensed in him yesterday. His raven hair, as black as the blackest midnight, had been brushed in the popular Titus style. It appeared he eschewed the current fashion of plastering his hair with scented pomade as a couple of rebellious ebony curls had fallen across his forehead.

She did not let his boyish appearance fool her.

This was a man aware of his power and position—

a man not to be crossed.

He'd tucked a folded newssheet under his arm. Probably to read in the coach as he did whatever rich nobles did with their days. Stopping at the foot of the bed, he scraped his inscrutable mahogany gaze over Grace.

She must look an absolute fright, and Grace self-consciously combed her fingers through her tangled hair.

He did not speak, though she detected disapproval as the silence stretched uncomfortably.

Was he waiting for her to speak?

To thank him for his grudging chivalry?

Well, he *had* saved her, and she *was* grateful.

"Thank you, my lord. For helping me escape Wyndam and bringing me here."

She sounded like a dying frog, and her throat ached something fierce.

Lord Renshaw remained stonily silent, and she dropped her gaze.

"If I might have paper and ink, I can write my friend. I am certain Joy and Dr. Morrissette will come around to collect me."

"You did not think to do that before causing the debacle you did yesterday?"

February snow was warmer than his tone.

How stupid did he think she was?

"Naturally, I did. Several times, in point of fact, my lord." Frost tinged her voice as well. "But Wyndam confiscated my correspondence."

Grace had been little better than a prisoner these last weeks. Nevertheless, she would not tell Lord Renshaw any more than she already had. He might've rescued her yesterday, but she did not owe this man an explanation.

Even if he was an aristocrat.

Turning her head, she coughed into the handkerchief.

Lord, she was miserable. All she wanted to do was slide down the comfortable mattress, burrow beneath the covers, and sleep. Instead, she must pen a pathetic missive to Joy and beg for help.

Grace peeked up at the earl.

Really, must he continue to stare?

Unkempt, in a strange house, ill, and obliged to him for coming to her aide, he must know he had her at a disadvantage. His silence was nothing short of rude, however.

He tossed the news sheets onto the bed.

They landed on Grace's calves and startled Ralph awake.

The affronted cat leaped to his feet and—after giving his lordship a disdainful glare, which the lord returned with an indifferent gaze—bounded off the bed.

Grace looked between Lord Renshaw and the papers twice.

"My lord?"

Sweat beaded her forehead and upper lip. She doubted the small fire crackling merrily in the hearth was the cause. Mrs. Goggin said Grace had a fever. That was what came from barely sleeping or eating for weeks and then dashing about in the pouring rain and getting splashed by carriages for hours.

Lord Renshaw rested a shoulder against the bedpost, and though he gave the illusion of languor, the muscle flexing in his jaw betrayed him.

He was livid.

The epiphany struck her with such surety she involuntarily fisted a hand beneath the sheet.

Unquestionably, perfectly in control, furious.

At her.

With a casual flick of a long, manicured finger, he pointed to the newssheet.

"I took the liberty of circling the text I thought you might find of particular interest, Miss Dooley. I assuredly found it…compelling."

A half dozen awkward blinks later
Still in the bedchamber

Grace did not want to read whatever Lord Renshaw thought she should. Instinct shouted that she wouldn't be happier than he at the content. Wary, she eyed him and then the papers.

His black eyebrows slashed together over his aquiline nose as he narrowed his eyes.

"You *can* read?"

"Yes." *Snob.* "Three languages fluently. French and German, in addition to English and a touch of Latin."

Grace was not certain why she shared that latter, except the earl made her feel beneath him. Inexplicably peeved, she seized the papers and swiftly perused the top one. A neat circle halfway down drew her attention.

Sanford, Earl of Renshaw, to wed housemaid.

Uh oh.

Grace stiffened, her mind denying what her eyes had read. Fingers fumbling, she searched the gossip rags and newssheets, easily finding the godawful headlines, thanks to his lordship's diligence.

Earl of Renshaw betrothed to mystery maid.
Ignominy surrounds the enigmatic Earl of Renshaw's secret betrothal.

No. No!

Eyes blurring with fury and shame-induced tears, Grace stopped after the third. Closing her eyes, she collapsed against the pillows.

What had she done?

Had Hollace Wyndam contacted the newspapers and fed them that claptrap out of a fit of vengeful pique at having been thwarted? She would not put it past the rotter. It did not matter who had notified the press; the damage was done.

"Oh, Lord," Grace whispered, mortified to her marrow. Horrified that in her desperation to escape Wyndam, she had brought scandal upon a complete stranger—a peer of the realm, no less.

"I sincerely doubt the Almighty cares a whit about that contrived drivel." No humor colored Lord Renshaw's voice. "I cannot say the same for *le bon ton*."

Grace had gone from one unholy predicament to another. Only this time, *she* was the villain. And it felt terrible, dirty, and unsavory.

What was more, an apology would do nothing to remedy the situation. She had besmirched an earl's reputation, yet he still acted the gentleman and aided a complete stranger.

Opening her eyes, Grace forced herself to meet his irate gaze.

"I sincerely beg your pardon, my lord."

She clutched the handkerchief in her fist. "I did not think—"

"No, you did not, Miss Dooley," the earl snapped.

His derisive laugh filled the room, a hollow and caustic reverberation. "Just yesterday, at my sister's wedding, I vowed that no scandal would surround my betrothal when I decided to marry."

"But we are not really betrothed. I can contact the papers and explain—"

"Explain what?" He cut her off again, his treacle-brown eyes sparking with ire.

"That you lied? You fabricated our betrothal? The truth matters not. Are you truly so gullible, so naïve, Miss Dooley, as to believe anyone gives a jot about the truth? Truth doesn't sell newssheets. Gossip, rumors, tattle, scandal, and disgrace does."

She could not argue against anything he said.

"I was not a housemaid but a companion to the elderly Mrs. Wyndam."

Grace did not know why she wanted him to know that insignificant detail. A servant was a servant to a man like him.

In a parting from his rigid self-control, incredulity sharpened his features. He would be a handsome man, breathtaking, in truth, if it were not for the perpetual sour and disapproving expression he wore.

"That matters naught. *You* are a commoner. A domestic. In service."

He made it sound like that made her a leper or a diseased harlot with French pox.

Never had Grace felt more inconsequential or insignificant. Less worthy or important. Defensiveness and anger flared at the earl's undeserved and undisguised scorn.

"I may not be a commoner." The words were out of Grace's mouth before she consciously processed the thought. She might be too. The truth of it was that her parentage was a complete mystery.

A hawkish and wholly skeptical eyebrow shied high on his forehead, fairly shouting,

"*Please. Do you expect me to believe that balderdash?*"

She lifted a shoulder. "I was raised in a foundling home. I have no idea about my lineage, but some of the girls there have been of the nobility."

Not for one minute did Grace believe she was one of them. For one thing, she was Irish. She knew that much. A letter had accompanied her to the foundling home along with monies to pay for her stay until she reached an employable age.

Lord Renshaw stiffened, suspicion pinching the corners of his eyes.

"*What* foundling home?"

"Haven House and Academy for the Enrichment of Young Women."

"Bloody, blasted…" He sent an infuriated glance upward. It was a wonder the plaster did not peel from the ceiling at the scorching glare. "Of all the rotted, deuced, confounded…*luck*."

She felt certain the last word was to spare her tender sensibilities.

A cadence of a thousand drums beating in her skull, Grace squinted at him. "Why?"

He ignored her question and, instead, jabbed a finger toward the scattered papers across her lap and the bed.

"Have you, Miss Dooley, any idea the harm your carelessly uttered words have caused?"

Yes. Yes, Grace did, but her remorse was little

comfort, and neither did it remedy the intolerable situation.

Shaking his head, his lordship paced back and forth at the foot of the bed, reminding her of a caged lion she had glimpsed once: Sleek, powerful, agitated, and angry.

"I received a summons from my father at half past six this morning." His lordship gave her a side-eyed glance, those whisky-brown eyes simmering with repressed indignation.

"And that is a bad thing?" Perhaps he did not get on with his father.

"My brothers are bidden by our father. I, however, have *never* been summoned before."

He took great pride in that. Grace could see it in his face and how he held his shoulders. Did that mean he was a man of character and integrity or a pompous twiddlepoop who rigidly complied with *le beau monde's* strictures?

Could he not be both?

As likely as snow in London in June.

"Why didn't you just leave me?"

He halted and spun to face her, puzzlement making the planes of his face more severe.

"What?"

"Why didn't you leave me then?" she repeated.

Grace searched his face for any sign that he recognized his part in the catastrophe.

"If you had, my lord, no one would've given any credit to a rambling maid's irrational declaration. But when you took me into your coach, you gave credence to the fabrication that there is something between us."

The earl's jaw worked as he clenched and unclenched his hands.

Grace eyed him warily.

Was he a violent man too?

Had she hopped from the proverbial pan into the fire?

"Do you presume to blame *me*?" The muscle in the earl's jaw practically bounced in his agitation. "Do you have even an inkling of what Wyndam intended for you?"

Of course, Grace did. Which is why she had fled in the first place.

She arched an eyebrow in response. She was perfectly capable of dramatics too.

"Are you serious, my lord?"

Of course, he was.

The man was incapable of flippancy.

"I risked enduring your wrath rather than Wyndam despoiling me."

Before Renshaw could respond, Mrs. Goggin swept into the bedchamber bearing a laden tray. "Seems to me you are partially to blame, your lordship. When your temper cools and your bruised pride heals, you will realize the truth."

Grace sent her a grateful glance but doubted Lord Renshaw ever acknowledged wrongdoing. He had probably been a dour child, afraid of his own shadow, and never did anything untoward.

Imagining him as a grave toddler eschewing his toys in favor of sitting like a perfect miniature gentleman prompted a smile, which she swiftly wrestled under control. She did not need Lord Renshaw thinking she was half-mad too.

Mrs. Goggin set the tray down. "Now, go see what

the Marquess of Trentholm finds so dire that he sent a messenger before the cock crowed and let this young lady rest."

"We shall resume this conversation when I return, Miss Dooley."

Lord Renshaw stomped toward the door, and it was a wonder he did not leave singe marks on the pretty green and burgundy Aubusson carpet.

Defiance sluicing her, tired of men dictating to her and threatening her, Grace angled her head. "I shall not be here."

Before she could blink twice, he spun about and marched back to the bed. Thunder etched his face, and Hades blazed in his eyes.

"You will be if I have to lock you in this chamber."

Grace gasped and shrank away from him. "You would not dare!"

Had she escaped one prison for another?

"My lord!" Mrs. Goggin gaped at her employer, clearly flabbergasted at his behavior. "Surely you jest."

"When have I ever jested, Mrs. Goggin?"

Grace could well believe the man did not possess a

single humorous, teasing bone in his large, well-muscled, overwhelming body.

Countenance grim, he faced his servant. "Lock the door and take the key with you when you exit this chamber."

"I cannot…" Mrs. Goggin objected, one hand at her throat and worry pleating the corners of her eyes. The side-eyed glance she slid Grace held an apology and trepidation.

"You can and you will." Lord Renshaw speared Grace with a wrathful glance. "If Miss Dooley disappears, I shall never be able to clear my name. I shall not have the Brockman name, the earldom, or the marquisate besmirched by disgrace. Until I contrive a solution, Miss Dooley remains here."

Did he hear himself?

"And an unmarried young woman confined to your home won't cause *any* gossip?" Grace said with such sarcasm that his eyebrows nearly took flight.

She did not know why she goaded him. Truly she did not. The earl brought out the worst in her. Mayhap it was her fever. She'd lost her ability to hold her tongue around the pompous prig.

But really.

Keeping a young woman against her will. If he thought lips flapped about his betrothal to a housemaid, imagine what they'd say about forcing an unchaperoned young woman to stay in his house.

He'd probably be lauded as a man about town; she would be ruined.

"No one but the Goggins and my coachman knows you are here, Miss Dooley. I intend for it to remain that way. Oh, and lest you think you can bribe them, each is loyal and will abide by my wishes, even if they do not agree with my reasons."

Another contrite glance from Mrs. Goggin as she poured a cup of tea confirmed the truth.

She would abide by her employer's dictate.

Grace had escaped one snare only to be captured in another.

She had been afraid of Wyndam, but his man… There was something imminently more terrifying about the Earl of Renshaw.

Arms crossed and lips pursed, she glared daggers at

the obstinate brute. It was a wonder he did not incinerate on the spot, so scorching was her glower.

She had escaped once.

She could do so again.

As if reading her mind, he pointed a finger, his raven eyebrows crashing together.

"You do not want to experience my wrath should you defy me, Miss Dooley."

"Pigheaded bully," Grace muttered beneath her breath.

"Also, obstinate, mule-headed, stubborn, inflexible, uncompromising…" Mrs. Goggins made no effort to whisper.

"Indeed." With a final scowl, Lord Renshaw strode from the room.

Pelandale House, Grosvenor Square
Thirty minutes later

The finely sprung coach rocked to a stop before the opulent Trentholm mansion. An intricate wrought iron fence on either side of the well-scrubbed stairs enclosed small patches of rich, verdant grass and rows of robustly pruned claret-colored roses.

For the first time in memory, Sanford had been called before his father, the Marquess of Trentholm, much like a child in a skeleton suit caught pilfering sweets from the kitchen. And he could guess why he'd received the early morning summons.

The confounded gossip rags.

How many underpaid sots had stayed up all night setting the small type for the tripe published this morning? How many of the upper ten thousand would gossip over breakfast at his expense and relish the pompous and haughty Earl of Renshaw's descent into scandal?

Oh, Sanford knew how Society viewed him.

Nevertheless, it was better to be considered a stuffy boor than a libertine or dissolute. What was more, and of significantly greater importance, he had managed to stay out of range of the gossipmongers' sights his entire adult life.

Until now.

Why had he played the gallant and, against his better judgment, taken Miss Grace Dooley into his coach? Mrs. Goggin had revealed the young woman's full name to him when she had told him his guest had awoken.

Though Sanford had known Miss Dooley meant trouble from the instant he'd seen her huddled on the coach floor like a street waif, an innate sense of decency prohibited him from leaving her to Hollace Wyndam's evil devices.

There'd been an inexplicable pull—an

indescribable connection from the moment their eyes met. Everything Sanford believed about honor, station, and reputation had been weighed against helping a defenseless woman who would surely have been despoiled had he not taken her with him.

In truth, Sanford's ire was not aimed exclusively at the woman lying in one of Hydeaway House's bedchambers. Miss Dooley had been right. Had he left her outside The Wicked Earls' Club, he would not find himself in this untenable position. The onlookers would've believed her deranged or an opportunist.

Honestly, he was not entirely sure she wasn't one or both.

He stared at Pelandale House's lobster-red front door for several long seconds, dreading the confrontation.

Egads, man.

Sanford Antony Edward Brockman, Earl of Renshaw, is not a coward.

No help for it. Better to get it over with and then return to Hydeaway House and deal with the attractive baggage he'd left fuming in bed.

As Sanford stepped from the carriage, his brother Ronan's much too cheerful voice rang out.

"So, Father has sent for the errant eldest son. How fortuitous that our dear papa arises at five every morning and reads the newssheets while he breaks his fast at the ungodly hour of six."

Bollocks.

Grinning like a deranged Cheshire cat *and* a cat in the cream, Ronan, the middle Brockman brother, fell into step beside Sanford.

"I thought I would offer moral support, old fellow. I have received an official summons from our illustrious sire dozens of times. I would be happy to give you a few pointers."

"I just bet you would," Sanford muttered, making no effort to conceal his ill humor.

He cast a baleful glance at the blue sky. All hint of yesterday's gale had passed, except for a few scattered puddles here and there. If it had not been for that blasted storm, he would not find himself in this uncomfortable predicament.

Ronan leaned in and whispered, "I have found it is

best to just nod and make affirmative sounds in the back of your throat until Father is done having his say."

Sanford snorted. "I do not need your advice, thank you."

"Nonetheless, I shall come along for moral support."

Something resembling a primal growl rooted around behind Sanford's breastbone in an effort to throttle up his throat. Naturally, being the singular Brockman brother with a modicum of decorum, he forbade the animalistic sound to emerge.

"Halloo."

His youngest brother, Benjamin, trotted up to meet them.

Bloody, holy…

Who else would deem it appropriate to intrude upon a private meeting?

Wearing a grin as gloating and imbecilic as Ronan's, he threw an arm around Sanford's shoulder.

"Never fear, big brother. We'll see you through this interrogation." He winked, the very devil in his gaze. "Ronan and I are quite the experts at this sort of thing."

Yes. Yes, they were.

Both had been naughty imps as children, and that unfortunate trait had carried into adulthood. Their sons, *and daughters,* would likely be adorable hellions too.

Amongst the brothers, Sanford alone had inherited staidness, whereas his rapscallion younger brothers had inherited penchants for precociousness and mischief.

They reached the top of the stoop, and Sanford looked between them, oddly touched at their brotherly, if somewhat misplaced, support.

"How did you know?"

"Rachael sent a note 'round an hour ago," Ronan volunteered.

Benjamin added, "She thought you might benefit from our company."

Leave it to their stepmama to watch out for him, even if Sanford did not need assistance.

"Do you suppose there'll be bets on White's books as to whether our dear brother will march down the aisle?" The wicked glint in Ben's eye suggested he hoped so.

Probably.

The *ton* gambled on anything and everything, from whether Mrs. Clutterbuck's excessive consumption of prunes might lead to another highly odiferous public incident to which young, athletic buck Mrs. Featherborne-Pinfield would choose as her next lover.

And bed to exhaustion.

"Assuredly," Ronan replied. "Mayhap also a wager as to whether the girl is increasing, hence the hasty betrothal. There are *so* many possibilities."

Sanford started to deny the latter, but with a sickening twist of his stomach, he realized he was not positive Miss Dooley wasn't with child.

His gut knotted tighter.

And if she was, would everyone assume the babe was his?

Bugger it.

Several foul oaths paraded across his brain, but he refused to give his brothers the satisfaction of seeing him lose control.

Ronan raised his nose and gave an exaggerated sniff.

Once. Twice. Thrice.

"Do you smell something offensive, Ben?" he asked with fabricated innocence.

"Indeed," Benjamin chuckled before he also sniffed in a manner worthy of a bloodhound. "Rotten fish." He sniffed again. "Or…God forbid! Is that *scandal* I smell?"

Ronan gave a sage nod. "Yes, by Jove, you have hit the nail head-on. Who was that arrogant blighter who said scandal is like fish gone bad? The stench remains a long while, blah, blah, blah…"

"Leave off," Sanford grumbled. "You have made your point."

In a moment of arrogance, he had said something to that effect when Ronan had married Mercy, and his brother had taken umbrage. For his stupidity, Sanford sported a black eye for a fortnight, courtesy of Ronan.

Fate must be having a grand laugh at Sanford's expense right now.

Likely the devil too.

Usually, disgrace followed a poor decision, not a chivalrous one. Sanford had gone and done the noble thing, and look where it had landed him? Had he walked away, his reputation would be intact, and he would not be in this deuced conundrum.

And Miss Grace Dooley would've been violently violated.

Her virtue for his pride?

It was nowhere near a fair exchange.

The truth of the matter was, Sanford had no idea what he was going to tell his father. It was highly inappropriate for Miss Dooley to remain at Hydeaway House. He assuredly was not going to pretend to be betrothed to the chit, despite the infernal flimflam in the papers.

Nothing would compel him to marry a member of the lower orders.

Nothing.

He rubbed the side of his nose as he and his brothers made the familiar trek to the study. The two bothersome bratlings prattled on about what dire punishment Sanford might expect.

"Father could cut off his allowance," Benjamin put forth.

"Do you receive an allowance, big brother?" Ronan

asked, his eyes wide and knowing full well Sanford had no need to do so.

A fresh-faced maid wielding a feather duster bobbed a curtsy as they passed.

Why, the solution was so simple as to be laughable.

Sanford could claim Miss Dooley was a newly hired maid to help Mrs. Goggin. Not that the perfectly capable and organized Mrs. Goggin needed anyone to assist her in tending the house.

But that did not explain the betrothal blather.

If only one person had heard Miss Dooley's ludicrous declaration, he might've explained it away as a misunderstanding.

The blustery wind and pelting rain distorted what she said.

She was in a feverish state and spoke delirium-induced gibberish.

Jealousy at having his maid leave his employ had prompted Wyndam's childish fabrication.

Unfamiliar nerves flitted around his midsection.

Buck up. Stiff upper lip and all of that rot.

Sucking in a steadying breath, Sanford rapped once

on the study door with the knuckle of his forefinger.

"Come."

Nothing in Father's directive or voice betrayed his mood a jot.

Sanford entered, and his irritatingly chipper brothers filed in behind him.

Father quirked an eyebrow, his gaze trailing from son to son to son.

"To what do I owe this honor?" he asked.

"We are here to lend Sanford moral support," Ronan volunteered, not bothering to hide his gleeful smirk.

"Aye," Benjamin agreed, just as obnoxious and cocky. "He's not accustomed to this sort of thing. Being the boring, perfectly behaved sod that he is."

A chuckle shook Father's shoulders as he leaned back in his leather chair and clasped his fingers together over his belly.

Well…that was unexpected.

And wholly welcome too.

The man before Sanford wasn't irate or outraged. Perhaps this was not such a conundrum after all. Trying to gauge his father's mood, he pulled an earlobe.

Rather than censure or anger darkening his visage, jollity twinkled in Father's gaze.

Sanford narrowed his eyes.

Was father making a May game of him?

Father's attention drifted to the neat stack of newssheets on the corner of his massive desk.

"I should have liked to have been informed before reading about your betrothal in the papers, Sanford. To a servant, no less. Never thought I would see the day."

Ronan and Benjamin burst into guffaws, laughing so hard that they had to hold onto one another for support. So much for help from that quarter, the immature asslings.

A grin pulled Father's mouth upward, despite his valiant attempt to keep a banal expression.

Devil a bit.

Father *was* poking fun at Sanford.

"When do we get to meet the lucky young lady?" his father asked, hilarity preventing him from keeping his voice steady.

"Pardon?" Sanford shook his head.

Surely, he had misheard.

He quickly clarified the situation. It was one thing to have *le beau monde* think he was betrothed to a servant and another entirely for his family to believe such balderdash.

"There is no lucky young lady. Well, there *is* a young woman, but we assuredly are not betrothed. It is a huge misunderstanding. She is merely a maid I hired—"

Holding his hand up, Father cut him off. "Parlor maid? Scullery Maid? Chambermaid? Maid of all work?"

Ronan and Ben erupted in gales of laughter again.

Queer in the attic blighters.

"Um, a maid of all work," Sanford improvised. "On a probationary period."

His countenance gone serious, Father leaned forward. All humor had fled, replaced instead by sobriety. "You will have to do better than that, son. Her social status is immaterial if there is a jot of truth in what the papers report."

"We are *not* betrothed," Sanford emphasized again.

"In a moment of desperation, she claimed we were. Hollace Wyndam would've forced himself upon her. I have no doubt he's the source of the newssheets' tattle."

"Where is the girl now?" Father asked.

Blast it.

He would get directly to the point.

"She is safe but quite ill. She caught a nasty chill. The physician has been to see her and assures me she should recover, but she cannot be moved at present."

That should satisfy his father.

"Does she have a name?" Father persisted.

Or not.

Sanford did not want to reveal Grace Dooley's identity.

"I shall wager a bottle of cognac that he's sequestered her at his cozy cottage." Ronan wiggled his eyebrows. "*That* won't cause any undue speculation."

Sanford chose to ignore his brother's taunting. "Naturally, she has a name, but I am reluctant to share it."

"Does it escape anyone how protective Sanford is of this mystery woman?" Benjamin added that morsel.

"I am protecting my reputation and hers," Sanford snapped.

Father pointed to an armchair before his desk.

"Sit down, Sanford, and let's hear the tale and see what can be done to curtail the tattle. After all, above all others, you have strived to keep your name off the gossips' tongues."

"Too late for that," Ronan put in merrily as he perched on the sofa's arm.

"Aye, far too late," Benjamin agreed, plopping onto the couch.

Settling into the chair, Sanford speared his brothers a glower. "There is no need for you to remain. Your *support*"—and lack thereof—"has been duly noted."

"I think they should stay." Father looked at each of his sons in turn. "They may have useful suggestions about how to handle this situation. A lot of people would enjoy seeing you taken down a peg—"

"Or three," Ronan quipped while waggling his eyebrows again.

"Or five," Benjamin offered with a cheeky grin.

Yes, Sanford was a stickler for rules and propriety. And yes, he spoke directly, not mincing his words, but he'd never been purposefully cruel. Nor had he ever teased, jested, or taken pleasure in someone else's misfortune as his family apparently thought appropriate in this situation.

Why it should rub him raw did not bear examining.

"It is comforting to know that my family holds me in such low esteem that you take pleasure in my distress." He stood, not missing the sudden exchange of troubled glances between his father and brothers. "I shall bid you good day."

"Now, Sanford. Do not take umbrage." Father also stood, placing his palms atop his tidy desk. "No one meant any offense."

"Didn't they?" He skewered each with an accusatory glower. "I beg to differ. Offense was exactly what was intended and accomplished."

His family knew Sanford had no sense of humor. Jollity was beyond him, for whatever reason. When, as a young child, he had realized his inability to be cheerful, silly, or frivolous, he'd accepted his oddness. Unfortunately, no one else had, and he was continually judged and ridiculed for his sternness.

Just once, he would like to respond with levity and lightheartedness, but the truth was that he was as incapable of doing so as a horse was likely to sing an aria. When he tried, his jests fell flat as an oatcake. Tamping down the ridiculous hurt he thought he had long since become immune to, Sanford rolled a shoulder to affect nonchalance.

"I suppose you believe I deserve this turn of events, but lest you forget, it is not just my reputation being bandied about, nor is it only my life that will suffer the consequences. I am fully aware that I am regarded as the bothersome pebble in the family's shoe, and perhaps I deserve a portion of the scorn and ridicule directed toward me. Nevertheless, in this situation, I had hoped for your support. That was a grave miscalculation on my part. One I shall not make again."

Devil take it, he sounded and felt like an intractable child.

"Sanford." Concern etched upon his features, Ronan rose and extended his arm. "We still need to figure out a plan. For your sake and the girl's. You must want to help her, or else you would not have saved her from whatever it was you saved her from."

Genuine chagrin pulled Benjamin's mouth downward. "I apologize, San. I was just having a bit of fun. Of course, we will do everything we can to help."

He veered a desperate glance at their father.

The truth was, Sanford had been a royal pain in the backside to his brothers regarding their choice of wives. It should come as no surprise they wanted their pound of flesh from him.

He stalked to the door, feeling the odd man out as he always had. He might hold a courtesy title and be the next Marquess of Trentholm, but Ronan and Benjamin had their father's affection and respect. Things Sanford doubted he would ever earn, no matter how hard he tried or how much it mattered to him.

Retreating into old, self-preservation habits, he schooled his face into a mask of neutrality and shoved his emotions to a fusty corner in his mind and heart to rot.

"I shall be staying at my house for the indefinite future." He skimmed his gaze over them. "And I shall not be at home to visitors."

"Ah, so the girl *is* there," Ronan said unnecessarily.

Sanford did not answer but took his leave.

He had a sick woman and a scandal to deal with.

Hydeaway House
Three nights later

"No. Stop. Do not touch me!" Grace shook her head and slapped the hand groping her. "I shall not be your mistress. I would rather die."

She tried to run—*God help me!*—but something had become tangled around her legs, holding them immobile. Fear choked her, making it almost impossible to draw air as she kicked and squirmed, desperate to escape.

Arms flailing, she arched her body, her heart beating so frantically it would surely burst.

Wyndam meant to ravish her.

He gripped her shoulders, shaking her.

"Nooo."

He would not easily force her. She would resist him until death if she must.

Grace swung her fist with all her might, taking great satisfaction in hearing the resounding *thwack* when she made contact with his cheek and heard his grunt. She cried out as pain exploded in her hand, yet she was not ready to give up the fight.

She balled her other hand.

"Let go, Wyndam, you bounder!"

Smack.

"Rotter."

Smack.

"Blackguard."

Smack. Smack

"Wake up, Miss Dooley." A concerned male voice penetrated the fog entrapping her. "You are having a nightmare."

That voice. It…was not Wyndam's.

Oh, thank God.

"Wake up," he insisted again in an urgent yet gentle whisper. "I am the Earl of Renshaw. Remember me? I took you into my carriage the other day."

Renshaw?

The grumpy, self-important boor?

The man Grace had claimed was her betrothed?

The curmudgeon who'd ordered her locked in her bedchamber?

Breathing heavily, her heart battering her ribs, Grace forced her eyelids open and shrank back into the pillows at the form hovering above her, the fire and shadows casting his face in a sinister mold.

The earl eased back, his expression equal parts vexation and relief.

He lifted his hand and made to touch her, but she winced and turned her face away.

"I am only going to check if your fever has finally broken," he said in a soothing tone as if she were a wild creature he feared would bolt or bite.

When she did not cringe away again, he gently placed the back of his hand on her forehead. The dim light made it impossible to tell for certain, but genuine concern appeared to radiate from his eyes. Dark stubble covered his face, and he wore only a shirt, the sleeves rolled to the elbows and exposing black hair-covered forearms, and ebony pantaloons which revealed sculpted thigh muscles when he moved.

She would wager her only piece of jewelry, a silver cross brooch that Mrs. Shepherd had given her, that very few people saw this starchy fellow in dishabille.

His blasted pride and all of that.

"Ah, yes. Excellent." He gave a sanguine nod. "I think it has."

"Where is Mrs. Goggin?" Grace asked, searching the room.

She wiped her palm across her damp forehead, her sweat-sodden nightgown clinging to her skin. She did not want to contemplate how she had come to be attired in the oversized, ruffled garment, which was likely the housekeeper's.

The earl rose and, after turning up two lamps that bathed the room in a soft golden glow, crossed to the washstand.

"She is asleep. I sent her to bed three hours ago. She's tended you without reprieve, and I feared she was on the verge of collapse. Then what would I do? She runs this household with the precision of an army officer and is irreplaceable."

He tipped his mouth upward in what Grace thought might be an attempt at a smile. "Plus, she tolerates my idiosyncrasies."

Was he trying to be humorous or glib?

If so, he had fallen short but in an endearingly awkward fashion.

But did that mean…?

Grace eyed him from beneath her eyelashes.

Had *he* nursed her these past hours?

She could not quite reconcile in her mind that the harsh man she had met in the pouring rain and who'd glared at her with thunder in his eyes as he threw newssheets on the bed, now tenderly wrung out a cloth.

"How long?" She swallowed, weak as a newborn pup. "How long have I been ill?"

"Three days. The physician has called twice daily." The earl glanced over his too-broad shoulder as he folded the cloth. "Do you remember our conversation from before?"

Graced nodded despite feeling bloody awful and frailer than she could ever recall. "It is not something one forgets. I have embroiled you in a horrible conundrum."

He did not refute her.

As Mrs. Goggins had, he poured her a glass of water.

Grace drank greedily before sighing and closing her eyes. "Please forgive me for being such an inconvenience. I never meant to impose upon you this long. I shall write my friends."

His answer was to gently swipe the cloth across her forehead and cheeks. "Later. You are not well enough to go anywhere at present."

Opening her eyes, her gaze locked with his.

The half-light muted his stern visage, and she could almost see the boy he had once been. Before responsibility and duty had leeched the joy from him. Or perhaps, he had never been cheerful and carefree but rather taciturn and severe even as a child.

She'd wondered about that before.

A couple of girls at Haven House had been like that. Always taking themselves seriously and critical of others' joy and laughter. It was no way to live life, with all of its hardships and trials. Mrs. Shepherd, the proprietress, had always advised her girls to seize joy and happiness where they might.

"Life is either a glass half full or half empty. Your perception, attitude, and thoughts determine your happiness," Mrs. Shepherd had said.

Forehead furrowed, Grace stared at the open door. "I thought I was to be locked inside this chamber."

Making a rough noise in his throat, the earl scratched his bristly jaw.

"I was not at my best when I said that. I assure you, you were never locked in. I beg your pardon for my ungentlemanly outburst."

"It is of no consequence," Grace said with as much lightness as she could muster. It was not as though she had been aware either way.

Lord, how she wished she could strip off this wet gown, but what would she put on instead? A swift examination of the room revealed no sign of the maid's uniform. Likely, Mrs. Goggin had taken the garment to mend and launder.

She shivered, and his lordship frowned.

"You are cold." The earl narrowed his gaze, sweeping it over her in a manner that ought to make her blush but instead caused a queer tingling in her middle that spread outward to her limbs. "Your gown is soaked through. You will need to change at once, lest you relapse."

His eagerness to see her well again caused no affront. After all, Grace had greatly incommoded the man. The sooner she was well, the sooner she could be on her way and done further inconveniencing him.

How had his interview gone with his father?

She did not dare ask, despite her avid curiosity.

"But what shall we use?" The earl scraped a hand through his already mussed ebony hair, then stood and planted his hands on his narrow hips. "I am not accustomed to keeping spare female clothing on hand."

Why that information should please Grace made no sense at all.

"There is no need, my lord. I shall be fine as I am."

For certain, Grace was not capable of changing herself, and she did not want Mrs. Goggin awakened. The sweet woman had been troubled enough.

A grin tipped the earl's mouth upward, and years of austerity melted away, leaving a devastatingly handsome man in its wake.

Good heavens. He's beautiful.

The Good Lord must've destroyed the mold after creating him, lest all females be reduced to gawping, tongue-tied featherbrains in his presence.

Grace tried not to gawk; she really did. But when he smiled, that flash of white teeth and a grin lighting his brown eyes, the Earl of Renshaw was irresistible.

"I have it." He snapped his fingers, looking well pleased with himself. "I shall be right back. You stay right there."

He pointed his finger, but not in the intimidating or demanding way he had a few days ago, but in an almost playful manner.

Besides, where would Grace hie off to in the wee hours of the morning, even if she could manage to stand without support? Which she was quite certain she could not. Sitting up in bed took every ounce of strength she possessed.

The earl strode from the room and returned in just

a couple of minutes carrying a long white garment. "I honestly have no idea where this came from. I do not wear them."

Grace was not surprised. Heat seared her cheeks at the unwarranted and uninvited imagery that sprang to her mind at his innocent admission. It must be the fever. What else could it possibly be? It had muddled her thinking.

"It is a nightshirt," he offered needlessly.

"Yes, I surmised as much."

Regardless, the devil would fart fairy dust before the earl helped her don the too-big garment.

Pulling his eyebrows into a puzzled vee, the Earl of Renshaw held it up. "It is too large."

"Indeed."

Grace could not be sure; however, a bruise appeared to already be forming on his angular cheek. Remorse coursed through her. She had never struck anyone before.

Sending her a triumphant grin, he plucked a pair of scissors from Mrs. Goggin's sewing basket sitting beside an armchair she'd situated between the fireplace and the bed. With surprising efficiency, his lordship snipped a foot off the nightshirt's bottom, leaving an uneven hem.

"If I roll up the sleeves, it should suffice," he said with a satisfied grunt.

Grace regarded the garment doubtfully. Her gown was only half the problem. The sheets were damp too. If he would leave the bedchamber, she could pull the blankets over the sheets and lay beneath the coverlet.

"I am perfectly fine as I am, my lord."

Thrusting her chin out at a mutinous angle, she folded her arms. In truth, she was not positive she possessed the strength to remove her nightgown and put his nightshirt on.

Draping the cropped garment over his forearm, Lord Renshaw puffed out an exaggerated sigh.

"I do not intend to ravish you, Grace."

"The thought never crossed my mind."

It hadn't.

The Earl of Renshaw might be pompous and arrogant, but he did not infuse her with fear for her virtue as Wyndam had. Renshaw was a true gentleman.

Something akin to gratification skittered across his face but disappeared so swiftly she might've imagined it.

"But as I have assumed responsibility for you," he said, "for the time being, I must insist."

"And I must refuse." Grace averted her gaze, then sighed. After all he'd done for her, he deserved an explanation.

"I am not being obstinate, my lord. In truth, I am not sure I can manage on my own, and it would be highly inappropriate for you to assist me."

"I can drape a blanket around you, tent-like, as you remove your gown, and I promise to close my eyes and avert my face as you don my nightshirt. Either you comply, Grace, or I shall be compelled to change you myself."

Her stomach dropped, and another chill swept over her, though her sodden gown mightn't have caused this shudder.

He did not jest.

An unflinching granite stare replaced the gentleness Grace had detected earlier. She had no doubt his lordship would see her nightdress switched if he had to sit on her to accomplish the task.

"You are a bully, Lord Renshaw."

"I have been called much worse." That muscle ticked in his jaw the merest bit, as it did when he held himself in rigid control.

"And I suppose you always get your way?" Grace would not win this argument, but this banter bought her a few more seconds of dignity.

"Not always, but more often than not."

She raised what surely must be dread-filled eyes. "Will you turn down the lamps first, please?"

"Of course."

After his lordship complied and procured the promised blanket for modesty's sake, Grace ducked her chin and fumbled with the row of buttons from her chin to halfway down her chest.

Blast, she was weak.

As frail as she was, she was not positive that she could lift her arms to pull them out of the sleeves. She was naked as a robin beneath the gown, and though she knew his lordship was right, she could not prevent a swell of resentment at his highhandedness.

"Are your eyes closed?" she asked, uncaring that petulance had crept into her voice.

"Yes, and I am looking away."

Was that amusement in his voice?

The rotten blighter—finding humor in her predicament.

"I am unbuttoned, and I have raised the gown to my waist, but I cannot lift it over my head," she whispered, mortified to her marrow.

"Clasp the blanket in front of you with one hand, and I shall help you with each arm in turn."

"You better not peek."

Or what? Grace couldn't even dress herself.

"On my honor, I shall not. I give you my word."

As she did not know the earl, his word meant nothing, but she supposed it might mean a great deal to a man of his ilk.

Head bent and blushing furiously, she complied.

With unexpected gentleness and care, he guided each of her arms from the sleeves and lifted the gown over her head. She held her breath, fearful the blanket would not stay in place.

"I shall slip the nightshirt over your head now."

She nodded, not trusting herself to speak.

A moment later, a cloud of fabric smelling of cloves and cedar settled around her shoulders. Again, he slid each arm into the sleeves, and once he was done, he cleared his throat, the sound rough and choked.

"Can you pull the hem down now, Grace?"

"Yes."

The earl was so close that she could feel the heat emanating from him. It beckoned to her chilled flesh, and she resisted the urge to lean into him and soak up his warmth. A peculiar tingling made her aware of him as a woman, which was the oddest thing.

She did not even like the man.

But she did not dislike him either.

In truth, the Earl of Renshaw rather intrigued her.

She shimmied the fabric over her hips and down her thighs with a few awkward wiggles. The effort exhausted her, and she sagged against the pillow, uncaring that the sheets were yet damp.

"I am done," she said tiredly. "I just want to sleep."

"Not yet." Lord Renshaw scooped her into his ironlike arms.

Startled, she gasped and clutched his shirtfront. "What are you doing?"

He strode from her chamber and down a narrow passageway, its walls bare.

Come to think of it, there were not any gewgaws or paintings in her chamber either. The house was as stark as the man himself.

"I am putting you in my bedchamber. I have no idea how to change bedding and even less desire to learn. You will sleep in my bed, and I shall sleep in the drawing room on the sofa."

A few moments later, he settled her onto his mattress.

Decorated in royal blue, forest green, and burgundy, his bedchamber bespoke a taste for the finer things without a trace of gaudiness. Grace would've expected heavy dark walnut furniture, but a cherrywood sleigh bed, matching armoire, and chest of drawers met her curious perusal. A full bookshelf nestled in the corner, an open book on the secretary beside the window, and three more tomes stacked on the nightstand indicated Lord Renshaw enjoyed reading.

After pulling the baroque Venice brocade bedspread to her chin, he brushed her hair off her cheek in a gesture so tender her breath stalled. He further surprised her by placing a chaste kiss on her forehead.

"Good. You are still cool to the touch."

Was that his only reason for kissing her?

Well, of course, it was.

What else would've prompted him to do so, though he might've used his hand again.

"I shall leave the door open in case you need anything," he said as if he had not just shocked her to her core. "The house is not large, so I shall hear if you call."

Why did a man of his station stay in an unassuming house like this?

Surely there was a familial home or two he might reside in.

His lordship turned to leave, but Grace impulsively grabbed his hand.

It was big and strong and warm, and the contact

caused a frisson to skitter from her waist to her neck.

"Thank you."

Facing her, he smiled again, a stiff upward sweep of his sculpted mouth. She could almost hear the creak of unused muscles, confirming it was not something he did often.

Why was that?

"You are welcome."

As always, his countenance remained inscrutable.

Nothing in his tenor revealed if his reply was automatic or sincere. That was the problem with this man—well, one of the problems. He was unreadable—always on his guard. She had never met anyone as capable of controlling his features, emotions, and tone of voice.

How awful it must be to never allow himself to relax, to be carefree and spontaneous.

"I am sorry I hit you." Grace was. She had no desire to cause him any further hurt or harm. In fact, the opposite was true, which bewildered her to no end. Her attention shifted to the purplish welt on his cheek. "I am afraid a bruise has formed and will be quite evident by tomorrow."

He lifted two fingers to the damaged flesh before he shrugged.

"It was not intentional. You were having a nightmare about Wyndam."

What, exactly, had she said while fighting the blackguard in her sleep?

Better not to know, or she would blush from her cold toes to her flushed hairline.

"People might question how it came to be." She would not have him suffer further on her account. He was not the monster she had first believed him.

"I shall claim to have walked into a door in my sleep."

Grace could not decide if he was serious or jesting.

He sighed, the slight sound almost carrying an air of disappointment.

Had he been joking?

Lord Renshaw's focus lingered on her face for an extended second, and Grace felt certain he wanted to say more. Regardless, he turned on his heels and strode from the chamber without so much as bidding her goodnight.

Long after his footsteps had faded and the house settled into the night's comforting silence, she lay staring at the burgundy canopy overhead.

Grace could not shake the sensation, almost a premonition, that when she'd climbed into Lord Renshaw's coach the other day, she had forever altered the course of her life.

And his.

Hydeaway House drawing room
Five days later – late afternoon

Legs crossed and with an open book, spine up, on his knee, Sanford unapologetically observed Grace dozing on the jade velvet sofa, her own book propped on her lap.

She wore his sea blue brocade banyan robe over her uniform to guard against the day's chill. The garment practically swallowed her. However, the color did astonishing things to those captivating blue eyes and her glossy raven hair lying in a thick braided rope over one shoulder.

He hadn't bothered with a jacket or neckcloth again today.

In any event, who would see him besides the

Goggins, Walton, and Grace?

The man he faced in the mirror each morning, who suddenly eschewed decorum and etiquette he'd strictly adhered to for over three decades, was a stranger to him. Nonetheless, a contentment Sanford had never known had come upon him, and he was loath to disturb the tranquility.

He was even more unwilling to acknowledge the source of his newly found serenity, even if she lay a few feet away. To do so would be to admit he had begun to care for the winsome baggage. Never mind that she was never far from his thoughts and for all of the wrong reasons too.

Given the rumors circling the upper salons regarding him and that he had not spoken a word to his family in a week, the past days should have been trying and stressful. Furthermore, he was no closer to resolving the betrothal debacle than he had been when Father had summoned him.

Except, he'd found that staying at Hydeaway House—he was not hiding per se—and avoiding the inquisitive stares of his peers was rather restorative. He had not even visited White's or The Wicked Earls' Club, though he had continued his daily ride through Hyde Park at seven in the morning rather than the fashionable hour when half the *ton* paraded forth.

It was no hardship to refuse invitations since he had not received any, presumably because they'd been delivered to Pelandale House. Or, perchance, he'd been deemed a pariah, and none were forthcoming.

Honestly, he did not give a fig which.

The upper ten thousand would eventually come 'round.

Earls and future marquesses were not in such abundant supply that Society would ostracize Sanford for long once it was known he was still very much available on the Marriage Mart.

According to Doctor Pritchard, Grace had recovered enough that she should be capable of traveling in a day or two. That information had not been shared with her as yet. Neither had she written her friends, though Sanford had promised she might when she had recovered sufficiently.

Having had days to ponder the situation, he had

decided there was naught else to do but allow her to leave. As no betrothal announcement would be published in the papers, no banns read, nor vows exchanged, the *ton* would be left to speculate as they were wont to do in any event. He would just have to bear the discomfort of the rumors until something more noteworthy captivated the *haute ton*.

The unexpected averseness burrowing around in Sanford's chest at the thought of Grace leaving made no sense. He had known her little more than a week, and she had been gravely ill half of that time. How could he have come to enjoy her company to such an extent that he'd considered hiring her as a maid?—for all of ten seconds.

Although Sanford had not revealed Grace's name to anyone, he feared Wyndam would, the bloody rotter. When her identity became known, she would become a target for the chinwags, libertines, and other unsavory citizens of London's underbelly, not to mention those smelling of expensive perfumes, swathed in silks and satins, and glittering with a vulgar number of jewels who enjoyed drawing blood the most.

Then there were the men…

He could not contemplate their behavior toward her without a murderous rage billowing up inside him. They'd consider her as no better than a dockside slattern.

In truth, it was a wonder Wyndam hadn't prattled off at the mouth already. Which probably meant Father had interfered and *encouraged* the bounder to remain silent. Either by buying up his vowels or threatening to reveal an unsavory secret that would destroy Wyndam.

Though by nature genial and fair-minded, Father could be utterly ruthless when it came to protecting and defending his family.

"Here we are." Mrs. Goggin arrived bearing a tea tray. "Tea and dainties," she proudly announced.

Sanford quirked an eyebrow as he examined the plentiful display. The tea tray had become more and more extravagant with each passing day. While the housekeeper always served tea when he was in residence, the afternoon pastime had never been this elaborate.

Clearly, Mrs. Goggin was much taken with Grace

(so was Sanford, truth be told) and meant to impress their guest.

Opening her eyes, a smile swept Grace's face. "Mmm. Do I smell ginger biscuits?"

"Ginger cake, miss." Mrs. Goggin beamed. "With whipped cream."

"Oh, my goodness. You are an absolute treasure, Mrs. Goggin. I shall grow quite fat on your delicacies."

"You could stand to add a little flesh to your bones, miss."

That was the housekeeper's mantra. Anyone who was not plump needed fattening up.

True, Grace possessed a slender figure, but she was delightfully rounded in the places a man appreciated. She swung her shapely legs over the sofa's edge and set her book aside. Under the distraction of the tea service being laid out, Sanford looked his fill. She wore no shoes, just stockings.

Grace had very nice legs and ankles, indeed.

In point of fact, she was a beautiful woman. As he'd learned since her fever had broken, she was also intelligent, witty, played the pianoforte and flute, liked animals, and was surprisingly well-read and adept at cards, chess, and archery, of all things. According to Grace, her cooking and baking skills needed improvement, although she could wield a needle with satisfactory skill.

In short, had she been of the nobility, he would've considered asking for her hand. No, he would have asked for her hand, for the truth was, such a remarkable woman would not last long on the Marriage Mart.

He would not have asked yet, of course.

One did not become affianced to a woman one had known a mere week, even if he might—probably was— falling in love with her.

Sanford rubbed his nose as Mrs. Goggin arranged the sandwiches, tarts, and biscuits. On second thought, many marriages of convenience and arranged marriages were, in fact, the result of swift betrothals and often between strangers. He was not opposed to such arrangements as a matter of course, but he would prefer a more compatible and companionable union.

But not to a servant, no matter how alluring her curves, how enticingly blue her black-lashed eyes, or how berry red her Cupid's bow mouth. And no matter that his heart ached with the emotion he felt toward her.

There was an established order to things: fish swam in the water, birds flew in the sky, and aristocrats married aristocrats. Commoners married commoners.

"Thank you, Mrs. Goggin." Grace lifted the Masons floral-patterned teapot with practiced ease.

"My pleasure, miss." With a bob of her head, Mrs. Goggin headed toward the door. "I have bread rising and partridge to prepare for supper."

Pausing, Grace raised eager eyes. "Would you like my help?"

It was rather endearing, her willingness to pitch in when most of the women Sanford was acquainted with were so accustomed to being waited upon that it would not occur to them to offer assistance.

She had been asking to lend a hand since she had left her bed, but the doctor had advised against it, and Mrs. Goggin would not hear of it. Even with an extra person in the house, she was more than capable.

Mrs. Goggin shook her head. "Deary, you enjoy being waited upon. You will be back to work before you know it."

She gave Sanford a behave-yourself look before she left, leaving the door wide open.

What did Mrs. Goggin think he would do?

Pounce upon Grace as Ralph, the dashed cat, was wont to do?

The notion was rather tempting, in truth.

If Grace were his wife, he could pounce upon her playfully anytime he desired. But she was not and would never be. So there would be no pouncing, tickling, or petting, more was the pity.

As the house wasn't large, they could hear Mrs. Goggin humming a hymn to herself as she puttered around the kitchen. A moment later, she burst into song.

Amazing Grace, how sweet the sound

That saved a wretch like me!

I once was lost, but now am found;

Was blind, but now I see.

Hmm, hmm, hmm…my heart to fear…

A pan rattled, and the oven door clunked.

With the drawing room door wide open, Mrs. Goggin could also easily hear Sanford and Grace. No chance of anything untoward occurring, for he hadn't a doubt that the housekeeper unabashedly listened to every word he and Grace spoke.

Likely, she cocked an ear for extended silences and would have no qualms about marching into the drawing room unannounced and wielding a wooden spoon if she suspected any hanky-panky, as she called it.

A couple of hours ago, Herman Goggin had left to run several errands for Sanford, including delivering a note to his father apologizing for his outburst.

It was not like Sanford to feel sorry for himself, nor did he brood on offenses. In truth, he could not put his finger on why he'd acted rashly. Self-control, staidness, adherence to strictures, and mindfulness of propriety and etiquette had always guided his life.

Until now.

From beneath half-closed eyes, he regarded the enchanting woman across from him.

Until her.

Grace poured their tea with a countess's finesse. She glanced upward as she added three sugar lumps to his cup.

"I need to write my friends, my lord. I am quite recovered now and do not wish to impose upon your hospitality any longer."

"I shall provide paper and ink after tea."

The words left a bitter taste on Sanford's tongue.

He had no choice.

Unless…

The idea popped into his head with the impact and ferocity of a cudgel blow to his skull. Blindsided and slightly dizzy, he could only stare at Grace for an extended moment.

Of course.

Why hadn't it occurred to him before this?

It was the perfect solution.

Well, not perfect, perhaps, but it would sure as Hades make him happy, and he believed he could make Grace happy.

She drew her winged ebony eyebrows together.

"Is something amiss, my lord? You look like you have taken a fright."

"Do you think you might call me Sanford, or if that is too informal, Renshaw?"

Grace set the teapot down and cocked her head like an inquisitive pigeon. "But you are a stickler for decorum. Besides, it would not be seemly."

"Only when we are alone," he persisted. Which he hoped would be very often. His blood sizzled at the thought.

Very often, indeed.

A fragile smile bent her mouth.

"Sanford, I shall be leaving soon."

"You do not have to leave, Grace."

9

At that, Grace paused, searching his face. Sanford could almost feel the wisp of her gaze brushing over him.

"But you know I must. Unless you require a companion?" she quipped, her indigo eyes dancing. "A maid?"

Sanford rose and, in two steps, closed the distance to sit beside her. Taking her hand in his, he grazed his mouth across the knuckles, pouring all of his unspoken emotion into the action. The skin covering the slight bumps was soft, the veins blue against her ivory skin.

Her expression grew pixyish with confusion as she gazed at their hands.

"I have no need of the sort of companion you are

accustomed to being." He rubbed his thumb across her knuckles. "However, I propose a different type of companionship."

Fiend seize it.

The right words would not come forth. Sanford had always been horrible at expressing warmer emotions.

"For a man who generally speaks directly and does not mince his words, I confess I have no idea what you refer to."

A wary expression erased Grace's earlier exuberance.

Just ask her.

"My lord?" Grace prompted, her ocean-blue eyes wide and her pretty lips parted.

"Sanford," he corrected.

His name on her lips… A simple thing, yet a precious gift.

"Sanford?" she complied, appearing adorably confused.

He kissed her wrist, then her nose.

When she did not recoil or slap him, he grew encouraged.

"We have much in common, and I think we are well-suited," he said. "I can provide you with everything your heart desires."

He rushed on lest she interrupt him, and he lost his train of thought.

"I know we haven't known each other long, but from the moment I saw you in the coach, I knew there was something extraordinary about you, Grace. I felt it deep within me—in the center of my very being." His dormant soul had been awakened, unfurling like a butterfly freshly escaped from its cocoon. "I never hoped to find a remarkable, extraordinary treasure such as you."

Not exactly poetry or flowery phrases, but Sanford had conveyed his sentiment without fumbling ineptness. He smiled, feeling rather foolish at expressing himself, but relieved as well. Grace alone could make him want to share his emotions—his innermost thoughts and dreams.

"I confess, you have completely captivated me, Grace, and I cannot fathom your leaving. I believe that we are meant to be together, that it was no accident that you sought refuge in my carriage."

His voice became oddly hoarse and gruff. "It was destiny, sweetheart. You and I. Us."

A winsome smile blossomed across her face, and adorable pink tinged her cheeks, but she met his gaze squarely. That was one of the things he most esteemed about her. No false modesty, feigned demureness, or artificial bashfulness.

Gathering Grace into his arms, Sanford lowered his head until their lips met.

Hers were soft and sweet and irresistible.

Every nerve in his body became alert, finely tuned to the soft, fragrant woman in his arms.

Sighing, she wrapped an arm around his neck and kissed him back. A shudder rippled through her, even as an electric jolt sluiced through him.

They would be so good together.

So bloody good.

Leaning her head against his shoulder, Grace gave him a tremulous smile.

"This is so surreal, Sanford." Her eyes glowed, and her voice grew husky. "I feel the same way but did not dare hope—"

"Then say yes, my darling."

If only she would agree, Sanford might truly be happy. Together, they could be exquisitely happy.

Please say yes. Stay here with me.

"You are...?" Grace swallowed, the slender column of her throat working, her eyes wide with wonder and joy as she roved her gaze over his face. "You *are* asking me to marry you?"

He went perfectly still.

What?

No.

Did she think…?

Perhaps he'd not been as eloquent as he had believed himself and certainly had not been clear about his intentions. Sanford had not mentioned marriage or even hinted at a union; he wished Grace to become his mistress.

His hesitation must've shown on his face because she snatched her hand away. Shoulders back, spine ramrod straight, and eyes flashing azure fire, she glared daggers at him.

"Marriage is *not* what you are offering, is it?"

Scorn and fury turned her voice throaty. And perhaps unshed tears too, for a sheen of moisture glinted in those gorgeous blue eyes. He would wager Grace would eat a hog farmer's boot leather before she allowed a single tear to escape, however.

"No. I cannot offer you…more." Sanford would not mislead her. "I thought because we get on so well—"

She threw a hand up, palm outward. "And I am without a position, so naturally, I would gladly hop into your bed. Willingly, eagerly, even gratefully become your *mistress*."

The word reverberated throughout the room like a gunshot, and he winced.

Sanford had made an unpardonable miscalculation.

See what stupid sentiments did?

That drivel made a man soft in the head.

Made him take impossible risks.

"It is not like that, Grace." He wasn't proposing a purely carnal relationship. "You *are* special to me. I swear, I have never kept a mistress before."

She snorted, a full-on, unladylike nostril exhalation

worthy of a winded equine.

Sanford adored her all the more for her hoydenishness.

"Am I supposed to feel honored?" *In truth, yes.* "Do you think your offer is any less insulting or degrading than Wyndam's, my lord?" *A great deal less.*

Each syllable cracked with contempt and offense.

"He would've forced me, but you think to entice me with promises of '*my heart's desires*?' My lord, you do not know what my heart's desires are."

Botched that to Hades and beyond.

"Grace, I…"

Sanford touched her arm. He must say something but could not fathom what would remove his foot from his mouth.

She jerked away, then stood, regal and magnificent in her wrath.

"My answer is no. Empathically, uncompromisingly, never in a thousand years, NO."

She tossed her braid over her shoulder.

"Have you an inkling how offensive it is that you deem me good enough to be your mistress but not your wife? I may be a commoner, but I shall never be any man's kept woman. Believe it or not, we baseborn have morals, pride, and integrity too. I know you believe those attributes are restricted to bluebloods, but I vow, there are more decent, ethical, and honorable plebians than aristocrats."

Why did Sanford want to applaud her?

Because she was right, in every respect.

Chest rising and falling rapidly with her agitation, Grace poked a finger in his direction. He suspected she itched to slap his face or punch him in the nose. "People like me must earn respect while you and your kind demand it."

A rapid succession of knocks resounded at the entry, followed by multiple footsteps and several exuberant voices.

Grace's attention flew to the doorway, and she paled.

Good God above. The housekeeper had no doubt heard every word.

"Your family is here," Mrs. Goggin called from the corridor, probably to spare Sanford and Grace a measure of chagrin. "I am kneading dough, else I would show them in."

Just bloody perfect.

"Sanford?"

Rachael.

"Where are you?"

Father.

"He's probably in the salon," Ronan said.

Sanford's written apology, delivered not more than two hours ago, had apparently,

prompted his family to descend upon him without notice.

All was forgiven, it seemed.

As one, he and Grace faced the drawing room door, just as Father, Rachael, Ronan, his wife, Mercy, Benjamin, and his wife, Isadora, plowed in. Curiosity, affection, and wariness shadowed their faces as they shuffled to a stop inside the doorway.

Grace gasped. "Mercy?"

"What, no Marissa?" Sanford craned his neck and made an embellished pretense of looking for his youngest sister behind the others.

Father shook his head. "She is shopping with a friend and sleeping over afterward."

If Corinna and the baron were not on their honeymoon, no doubt they'd be here too.

"Grace." Mercy rushed to embrace her girlhood friend. "I had no idea you were the mystery woman I have been hearing about for nigh on a week now."

"And I did not realize you were married to Lord Renshaw's brother." Grace sliced Sanford an accusatory glare.

Mercy faced her husband. "Ronan, this is Grace Dooley. I have spoken of her often."

"And so you have, my dear." Ronan bowed. "A pleasure, Miss Dooley. What a coincidence that you and my wife were raised in the same foundling home."

"Indeed," Father said dryly, pointing an accusatory stare at Sanford. "One has to wonder why you failed to mention that fact, son. Unless you were not aware."

Sanford held his tongue.

This was uncomfortable enough without trudging down another bumpy path.

"Ah, you did know," Father said, censure in his

modulated tone.

Another first directed at Sanford by his sire.

Rocking back on his heels, Father grasped his lapels.

"By the by, Wyndam will not be a bother to either of you again." His attention veered to Grace before settling on Sanford again. "I *persuaded* him it was in his best interest to leave town for a while. Without him adding fodder to the fire, the tattle should settle soon enough."

Benjamin made a great point of examining Sanford's bruised cheek. He pointed at his unmarred face. "Zounds, whatever happened to your cheek, big brother?"

Before he could respond, Grace said with an artificially sweet smile, "I slugged him in my sleep."

Lord, that sounded bad.

At her honest admission, six pairs of eyebrows flew to hairlines.

"She was having a nightmare," Sanford rushed to explain. "I tried to comfort her."

Devil and damn.

That sounded worse—as if they'd been sharing a bed. In point of fact, to be absolutely truthful, Grace *had* slept in his bed the one night. There'd be the devil to pay if she mentioned that.

Every eyebrow stayed elevated, but his brothers grinned. Mercy's and Isobel's mouths went slack, Rachael's eyes narrowed in speculation, and Father pulled his mouth into a grim line as disapproval flashed in his eyes.

From bad to worse to scandalous in less than two *tick-tocks* of the blue marble and brass ormolu mantel clock.

"We must have tea soon and catch up, Grace." Mercy's no doubt deliberate change of subject dispelled the awkwardness to a small degree.

A very small degree.

Grace curved her mouth upward as well. "I would like that."

Fashionable in a cerulean-blue and ivory gown and spencer, Rachael continued into the room. Concern flitted across her face as she glanced between Sanford and Grace, her gaze lingering on the banyan for a long second.

One might read all sorts of inferences in Grace wearing Sanford's robe. Particularly after the previous troublesome remarks.

"We are interrupting," Rachael said, consternation puckering her usually smooth forehead.

It was not a question.

Did no one realize introductions had not taken place?

Had everyone tossed civility out the window?

"Nothing of import, my lady." Grace dipped into a perfect curtsy. "I have just refused to become Lord Renshaw's mistress. I have a letter to write so I might quit this house with all possible haste to keep my reputation and virtue intact."

Sanford's family turned appalled gazes upon him, and shame, unlike anything he had experienced, tunneled through his veins and set his face aflame. At that moment, he rather loathed himself. It would've been better to have let Grace leave his life than insult her beyond forgiveness.

She touched Mercy's arm. "I hope Joy Morrisette

and her husband will take me in for a time."

Father made a rough sound in his throat.

"Nonsense." Mercy shook her head. "You can stay with Ronan and me. I insist upon it. Our house has plenty of room, even with our girls."

Ronan had been named guardian to two orphans. That was how he and Mercy had met. She had been their governess.

"I should hate to impose." Grace appeared hopeful and simultaneously embarrassed.

"No imposition whatsoever, Miss Dooley. Mercy can help you pack, and you can accompany us when we take our leave," Ronan said.

Sanford stabbed him a look that shouted, *Traitor. Betrayer of brothers.*

Ronan simply grinned.

"I have very little to pack. I shall not be above five minutes." Grace met Sanford's eyes. Hurt, betrayal, and, yes…something warmer and infinitely precious glowed in hers too.

"*I feel the same way—*" she had said.

Did she love him?

Did it matter?

Yes.

No.

Sweet Jesus, who was this confused, feckless, double-minded bottlehead?

Sanford opened his mouth, then closed it with an audible snap.

What could he say?

Especially in front of his transfixed family?

I am a jackanape? A maggot-pated rotter? An unthinking, selfish boor?

You are far too remarkable and wonderful and dear to be any man's mistress?

Be happy, my darling?

His only chance for happiness was about to walk out of his life, and there was not a dashed thing he could do to prevent it.

There is one thing, his infuriatingly straightforward conscience insisted.

No. Absolutely not.

It was unthinkable. Preposterous. Inconceivable.

Sanford *could* not.

He could not ask a common maid to be the next Countess of Renshaw.

He'd be the laughing stock of not only his family but the entire *le bon ton* as well.

Yes, his cursed pride kept his mouth firmly shut as he watched the only woman he had ever loved turn her back on him. Cutting his heart from his chest with a rusty, serrated knife would've hurt less.

And yet, he would let her go.

With the poise and majesty of a peeress, Grace swept from the room, and Sanford knew beyond any doubt that he would never recover that part of him she took with her.

10

Ronan and Mercy Brockman's Home, London
A week later – Early afternoon

Curled into the corner of the lavender and beige-toned settee in Mercy and Ronan's comfortable drawing room, Grace stared blankly at the newssheet in her lap. A moment ago, she'd glared so hotly at another nasty story in the paper speculating about the identity of Lord Renshaw's *secret* love, it was a wonder the paper hadn't incinerated.

Really.

Had people nothing better to do than conjure tattle?

Lord Trentholm had assured her and Sanford that the prattle would lessen with Hollace Wyndam gone from London, but when?

As grateful as she was for her friend's hospitality,

this arrangement must be temporary.

Not only because Mercy was increasing, and soon they'd need to transform the bedchamber Grace used into a nursery, but because the chance of encountering Sanford could not be ignored. This was his brother's house, after all. Although she had the impression that the brothers were not terribly close.

Grace meant to visit the employment registrars and submit her resume; if she could borrow the Brockmans' coach, that was. She had perused employment postings in the newssheets this past week, but most positions she qualified for required letters of reference from one's most current employer, which she did not have and could not get.

Nevertheless, she still possessed letters from Mrs. Shepherd and her first position as a companion. Hopefully, those would suffice, but if not, she could impose upon Dr. Morrisette and Ronan to write her letters of character.

Touching her chin with her forefinger, Grace narrowed her eyes in contemplation. "*Hmm.* I wonder if a position is still available at Balderbrook's Institution for Genteel Ladies?"

Another friend from Haven House, Chasity Noble, now Chasity Terramier, had worked at the girls' school and some time ago had invited Grace to apply as an instructor. It couldn't hurt to write Chasity.

You are not completely undone, Grace Alexandra Marina Shepherd Dooley.

You are intelligent, resourceful, and healthy, and you have loyal, supportive friends. You shall overcome this, and one day you shall look back and realize you are better for having endured it.

The self-talk did little to bolster her spirit. Grace would rally, though. In time. It was not her nature to mope or sulk.

Smothering a yawn—she had not slept through the night since leaving Sanford's—she unfolded her legs before setting the papers aside. The earlier rain shower had passed and, arching across rooftops in a glorious colorful display, a rainbow had formed.

Weren't rainbows supposed to represent hope?

A promise?

Truth be told, Grace's usual optimism had gone

missing, and Sanford was to blame.

No, becoming enamored of him was the cause. She had barely even permitted herself to acknowledge her budding sentiments. In her heart, she'd known it was impossible.

But when he had made his fervent declarations, he'd seemed so sincere and genuine that joy had infused her, and in her innocence, she had stupidly jumped to the wrong conclusion. And been mortified to her core.

Nincompoop.

Regardless, there was no time like the present to venture to the agencies. Wallowing in self-pity never benefited anyone.

"Lady Trentholm has invited us for tea this afternoon, Grace."

Mercy glided into the room, holding a note. The current fashion hid the gentle swell of her belly, but soon her pregnancy would be noticeable. "I hope you will say yes. You have not left the house since arriving."

Grace stood and shook out the skirts of her borrowed teal-hued morning gown. Mercy had lent her three gowns, as Grace had nothing but the pilfered maid's uniform. Sanford said he had sent for her things, but either Wyndam had chosen to ignore the request, or he had disposed of them.

Probably the latter.

"That is kind of her ladyship, but I cannot think it wise." And why would a marchioness invite a disgraced servant to tea? No, best to refuse the offer and steer clear of any more scandal sheets.

Besides, Sanford might've returned to the familial home.

As if she had read Grace's mind, Mercy glanced at the letter again.

"Rachael says she does not expect Sanford. He's remained…ah…*elusive* since you departed." She wrinkled her nose.

"His family is worried about him, Grace. He's eschewed all of their attempts to see him."

Why?

Embarrassment or self-righteousness?

Or was it possible he suffered too?

Mercy glanced up. "Rachael believes he's mortified about how he treated you. Sanford has always maintained a stellar reputation, never flirting with anything remotely unsavory or questionable. Offering you hospitality in his home was way outside the bounds for him."

"I…" What could Grace say to that? "I am responsible for the gossip in the papers, but he was still kind to me."

More than kind.

Gracious, generous, considerate…

There had been a spark, an awareness, an intricate weaving of their spirits, and in another time and place, they might've been able to build a contented life. Circumstances had brought them together for a time, but now they must go their separate ways.

Disappointment and pain seared Grace's heart. Sadness and heartache shrouded her, and she dropped her gaze lest Mercy detect the tears forming in her eyes.

Mercy crossed the distance between them and took Grace's hand.

"I am a good listener if you want to talk about it, dearest. I also can keep confidences, even from my husband, should you ask me to."

And Grace did want to talk about it. She and Mercy had been like sisters at Haven House. Perhaps getting another person's perspective would help her broken heart heal. Or, at the very least, give her direction.

Sighing, she resumed her seat, and Mercy sank to the cushion beside her. In short order, Grace recounted how Sanford had rescued her, her panicked public statement about them being betrothed, her time at his house, and her feelings for him.

"I did not think it was possible to fall in love so quickly." A tear slid down her cheek, and she shook her head in self-castigation. "I scoffed at such claptrap, but when it happens to you…"

She shrugged and, with a watery smile, accepted the lace-edged, floral-embroidered handkerchief Mercy slipped her.

"I feel like an utter fool, Mercy."

Grace stared out the window. A double rainbow glowed brightly beyond the panes now. She swallowed, the ache in her throat nearly choking her. Voice small and throat tight, she confessed, "I thought…" Even now, her naivete galled her. "I thought the earl was asking me to marry him."

Sighing, Mercy wrapped an arm around Grace's shoulder.

"Sanford is a complicated man. I shall not pretend that I understand him. I do not think Ronan does either. The earl adamantly opposed Ronan's marrying me and Benjamin marrying Isadora. Oddly, their parents embraced the unions, so whatever prejudices Sanford had, they were his own, whether self-contrived or adopted. He adheres to a rigid, self-imposed moral code, and I fear it will cause him much pain."

Grace summoned an artificial smile. Marshaling her fortitude, she declared, "I have only known him a fortnight. Surely, it shall not take long for my heart to heal."

Wouldn't it?

Was love measurable in degrees or by time?

One either loved completely and utterly, irrevocably and unconditionally, with one's heart, mind, soul, and spirit, or one did not. And as she had so brutally learned, sometimes love was not enough.

It could not compete with pride.

"I loathe seeing you sad." Mercy gave her a little hug. "Say you will come to tea. The Brockmans are truly endearing. I think you will like them."

"Yes, I think I shall go." It might do Grace a world of good.

Or it could prove disastrous, but in either case, at least it would take her mind off Sanford for a short while. How long, exactly, did it take a broken heart to mend?

"I was going to visit the employment registrars today."

What difference would another day make?

"We can do that tomorrow." Mercy stood and patted her tummy. "I have shopping to do for the baby, and Bellamy and Arabelle want to come along and help. I promised them ices at Gunter's too."

Delightful, well-mannered children, the sisters could not wait for the babe to arrive. And to think, Mercy had been their governess before she and Ronan had fallen in love. Of the three Brockman sons, Sanford alone deemed himself too superior to marry beneath him.

Several of Grace's closest friends from Haven House and Academy for the Enrichment of Young Women had married, and a few had married remarkably well. Made brilliant matches, truth to tell.

Grace would not be among them.

At least it wasn't something she contemplated yet. Mayhap not for a very long while. Her heart had set itself on a certain tall, black-haired, whisky-eyed lord, and he'd taken possession of the organ, whether he wanted it or not.

Standing and stretching her spine, Grace bent her mouth into her first genuine smile of the day. "Yes, that sounds splendid. What time do we leave for tea?"

"Three." A smile lit Mercy's pretty face. "I am so happy you have agreed."

Grace glanced downward at her gown.

"And, yes, your gown is perfectly acceptable," Mercy said, angling toward the door. "It is a private family tea without all the pomp and ceremony."

"And you are certain Sanford..." *Blast and blisters.* Despite the heat skating up her cheekbones, Grace strove to keep her features neutral. "That is, Lord

Renshaw will not be there?"

"It is highly unlikely, according to Rachael. Despite numerous invitations, he has not returned to Pelandale House or been seen in public since you left."

Had Grace's departure impacted Sanford as much as it had her, or was he nursing a bruised ego? How she wanted to believe it was the former but suspected it was the latter.

11

Grosvenor Square, London

Four o'clock that same afternoon

With a start of surprise, Sanford glanced up and realized the miles he'd blindly walked these past hours had led him to Grosvenor Square.

To Pelandale House, to be precise.

To home.

Despite everything—his anger, chagrin, frustration, and yes, even his pulverized heart, he needed his family.

He'd spent a week avoiding them, the *haute ton*, White's, The Wicked Earls' Club, Tattersalls, and even his morning rides in Hyde Park. The truth was that when Grace walked out of Hydeaway House last week, he had sunk into a profound case of the blue devils.

Another first for him.

He could not eat, sleep, bathe, or even drag his sorry arse to his bed. The first three days, he'd remained in the salon and drowned his pain and sorrow in cognac. Until the Goggins had refused to supply him with another drop.

Pesky, nosy, caring busybodies.

He ought to turn them out onto the street without reference for their impudence. The old Sanford might've briefly considered it. The new man recognized their impertinence for what it was: affection.

A week spent in introspection—and not liking what he had learned about himself—had compelled him outdoors, lest he go mad with self-loathing.

Gazing up at Pelandale House, he battled conflicting emotions.

The desire to surround himself with those he loved and who loved him in return, and the absolute conviction he was unworthy.

Rolling his shoulders, he skewed his mouth into a sardonic smile.

Might as well go in.

He was here, after all.

These past days, he'd realized that he was a bloody, pompous sod. He owed his brothers and their wives an apology.

When had he become such a self-righteous, opinionated, unyielding blighter?

When had he elevated himself and his beliefs and values above others and become a condescending assling?

He owed Grace—*my dearest heart*—an apology too.

Was she still at Ronan and Mercy's?

Should he pay her a call?

Would she receive him?

No, better to pen her a note and beg her forgiveness.

Sanford did not dare hope for more.

After buttoning his rumpled jacket, he scraped a hand through his hair in a futile attempt to comb his windblown (and unwashed) hair. Climbing the spotless stairs, he grazed a hand over his unshaven face. He looked around furtively, quickly sniffed beneath his arms, then wrinkled his nose.

Good God above.

Decidedly off-putting.

He had never appeared in public this unkempt and odoriferous and would've scoffed at any suggestion he would ever do so. Nevertheless, here he was, resembling a rakehell coming off a week-long binge.

What was more astounding, Sanford did not give a tinker's curse.

Of one thing, he was certain. His family would accept him as he was. Hadn't they done so these many years, even when he did not deserve it?

Heaving a sigh, he let himself in.

"Good day, my lord." Sturges, the butler, silently appeared out of nowhere as butlers were wont to do.

To his credit, the servant's expression did not alter a jot as he took in Sanford's disheveled appearance. However, his nostrils may have twitched before he commandeered them into commendable stillness.

Muted laughter and chatter carried to Sanford from the drawing room.

A glance at the longcase clock revealed it was tea time.

"Private tea today?" Sanford would leave if guests

were present.

It was one thing to intrude upon his kin looking and smelling like a mangy street mongrel, but another if his presence exposed them to ridicule or became more gossip fodder.

"Indeed, sir."

Kindness brimming in his gaze, Sturges gave a sympathetic nod.

Likely as not, the servant knew exactly what had transpired at Hydeaway House. Servants always did. It was rather uncanny and not a little disconcerting.

"Do you wish to freshen up before joining them?"

The broad hint did not go unnoticed.

However, Sanford did not want to, even though his bedchamber contained a number of suits, boots, neckcloths, and so forth. In truth, he hadn't the energy, though Brewster would assist him and could have him bathed, shaved, and garbed in fresh clothing in fifteen minutes.

That is, if the valet did not swoon or have an apoplexy upon seeing Sanford in his present state.

"I know I should, but I shall not." He offered a half-rueful, half-depreciatory smile.

"I shall request a hot pot of tea and sandwiches," Sturges said, no condemnation in his wise gaze. "Perhaps cold meat and cheese too?"

This morning, a glance in the looking glass revealed that Sanford appeared gaunt and half-starved. Mrs. Goggin was nigh on to having a paroxysm because he had barely eaten this past week.

Love was a wondrous, awful, exhilarating, torturous paradox.

It had brought him, the top-lofty Sanford Antony Edward Brockman, Lord Renshaw, to his knees.

"I would appreciate it, Sturges."

Sanford pulled his waistcoat into place—*what is that stain from?*—and made a half-hearted, if completely futile, attempt to straighten his limp-as-wet-straw neckcloth.

"Very good, sir." Sturges fell into step beside him, his focus straight ahead, then asked, "I presume you want to announce yourself?"

The servant knew him well.

"I would."

Just in case Sanford was not as welcome as he anticipated.

With a nod of understanding, the butler veered down a side corridor as Sanford continued onward.

Unfamiliar trepidation assailed him. Filling his lungs, he entered the drawing room.

And stopped dead in his tracks.

His heart toppled over itself, and he flashed hot, then cold, then hot again.

Grace.

My precious love.

How could she be even more beautiful than he remembered?

Arranged in a simple but elegant chignon, her silky jet-black hair shone, and her gorgeous eyes… Those eyes could compete with the deepest ocean's blue.

Chintz china teacup in hand, her eyes widened, and the color leeched from her face except for two bright crimson spots on her cheeks. Her pulse jumped at the juncture of her long, elegant throat and collarbone, a turbulent testimony to her discomfit.

Hand shaking, she fumbled with the cup, placing it upon the tea table where it rattled in its saucer and tea sloshed over the brim.

The room descended into pregnant silence, made worse by his family's inquisitive stares boring into him with the intensity of hot pokers.

Idiotic of him to have not considered she might be here. Ronan and Mercy were not likely to ask her to remain at home while they enjoyed tea with the marquess and marchioness.

Sanford's gaze locked with Grace's, and everything faded until nothing else existed but the two of them. His soul cried out to hers, craving the completeness only she could provide.

Give me another chance, he silently begged.

He could not have looked away if his life had depended upon it.

Then everyone began talking at once.

"Sanford, dear. Do have a seat." Her face wreathed in a strained smile, Rachael exchanged a confounded glance with Father. "I shall ring for more tea."

"Sturges has already gone to the kitchen," Sanford said.

"My boy, I am so glad you have come." Compassion and affection crinkled the corners of Father's eyes as he moved to pump Sanford's hand and clasp his shoulder.

"Have you been wrestling with bears? Or hogs?" Ronan quipped, never missing an opportunity to harass his older brother.

"Hush, darling," Mercy gently chastised. "Now is not the time to tease your brother. Surely you see he's not himself?"

Praise God for that.

Sanford never wanted to return to the unbearable snob he'd been.

Marissa ran to embrace him and then wrinkled her nose.

"*Eww*, Sanford. You smell."

"You look bloody awful, old chap." Benjamin also clasped his hand.

"Be kind, Benjamin," Isadora admonished.

Sanford gave her a grateful smile, which she returned with a jaunty twinkle in her eyes.

He'd misjudged her and Mercy. Badly.

Benjamin grinned, though not unkindly. "Well, he does, darling."

Corinna swept to his side and, without hesitation, embraced him. She was made of sterner stuff than Marissa. "I am glad you are here. Now the family is complete."

When had she returned from her honeymoon?

His new brother-in-law, Caspian Graystone, Baron Strathmore, slapped his back and gave him a conspiratorial wink. "Good to see you."

Grace alone remained silent.

Clasping his hands behind his back to keep from bolting to her and pulling her into his arms, Sanford cleared his throat.

"I owe all of you a sincere and heartfelt apology. I have done much soul-searching this past week and concluded I have been an unforgivable, judgmental prig."

Surprise, guardedness, and approval skittered across his family's faces.

He met Mercy's and Isadora's gazes, shame pricking his conscious.

"Mercy and Isadora, my behavior toward you has been unpardonable. I hope in time you might come to forgive me."

Both angled their heads in confirmation, though neither spoke.

His brothers shared a speaking glance as they wrapped an arm around their wives' waists in mutual protective gestures. That might've been Sanford and Grace had he the character and fortitude his brothers possessed. They had chosen to cock-a-snook at society and reaped a lifetime of rewards for doing so.

As if sensing how difficult this was for Sanford, no one interrupted him.

He shifted his attention to Grace, sitting statue-still, hands clasped so tightly in the lap of her teal gown that her knuckles showed white.

"Most of all, Grace, I humbly beg your forgiveness.

You are the single best thing that has ever happened to me. That day you hid in my coach was the day I began changing—hopefully for the better."

A concert of emotions played across her countenance, yet she did not speak.

Because this was not a conversation one had with an audience.

As per his usual ineptness, Sanford had mucked that up too.

He glanced around the room.

"Might I have a word in private with Grace?"

Apprehension flitted across her delicate features, and Sanford feared she would bolt.

"Just a few moments. Please." He was not too proud to beg. Not anymore.

She replied with a short, terse nod.

Thank God.

"*Ahem*." Father loudly cleared his throat. "I say, Rachael, didn't you mention a new rose was blooming in the garden?"

Confusion swept across Rachael's face.

"Roses do not bloom in… Oh." Comprehension dawned, and she darted a glance toward the garden windows. "Erm, yes. I believe I may have mentioned it in passing."

Bless her.

"Let us take a look, shall we?" Father encouraged, his arm extended toward the door.

"Oh, yes, let's do," Ronan drawled, not even trying to conceal his drollness.

With a serene smile upon her lips, Mercy elbowed him in the ribs.

"*Oomph.*" Chuckling, he rubbed the offended area.

Corinna rolled her eyes as she slid her hand into the crook of Strathmore's elbow. "You are about as subtle as a purple pig wearing a poke bonnet, Papa."

Leave it to Corinna to state the obvious.

"A purple pig?" Marissa giggled as she sauntered to the door. "Lady Pinkersham-Babott has a white poodle she dresses in a pink jumper. Poor thing has pink bows tied to its ears and tail too."

"You can tell us all about Lady Pinkersham-

Babott's poodle in the garden, Marissa." Rachael shooed everyone before her, like a mother hen herding her chicks.

The door closed behind her with a soft snick.

Grace lifted her chin, proud and magnificent.

"You have exactly two minutes, Lord Renshaw, and then I am joining your family to look at the nonexistent rose."

12

Still in Pelandale House's drawing room

Exactly ten tense heartbeats later

Grace forced a mien of calmness over her features. Her heart battered her ribs, and her blood crashed through her veins like a storm surge. It had taken all of her equanimity to sit calmly when Sanford entered the drawing room.

It made no difference that everyone was as flabbergasted as she was at his unexpected arrival. He looked simultaneously awful and wonderful, and despite the way they'd parted, she longed to run into his arms.

Expression guardedly hopeful, he approached, all lithe masculine grace.

Must he be so dashed handsome? So virile?

Endearingly rumpled, Sanford kneeled beside her and gazed at her without speaking. The strong column of his throat worked beneath his shoddy cravat, as if he struggled to find the right words.

Against her better judgment and notwithstanding the wisdom screaming caution to her, she could not prevent herself from touching his scruffy jaw. Dark stubble covered his face.

"You look as if you haven't eaten, shaved, or slept in days," she said softly, tenderness and love for this man overcoming her. Even now, when he had rejected her so cruelly, she could not deny him comfort.

Closing his eyes, he raised his hand to press her palm against his cheek. A shudder rippled through him, sending a jolt of awareness careening through her.

"I haven't." His voice emerged in a gravelly rasp. He opened his eyelids, capturing her gaze with his turbulent eyes.

So much emotion simmered there that she caught her breath.

"I miss you, Grace. Desperately."

Her heart skipped a beat and then pounded an

irregular rhythm, making it impossible to breathe evenly. To think clearly or rationally. She'd missed him too—Lord, how she missed him—but not enough to fling her self-respect, morals, and integrity aside.

Stiffening her resolve, Grace tamped down her love, forcing it to a dark corner and withdrew her hand. A person could only take so much before they shattered.

"What is it you wished to say to me, Sanford?" She tossed a frantic glance at the clock. "You only have a minute left."

It was his turn to skim his fingers across her cheek.

Grace clenched her jaw and curled her toes in her shoes to keep from leaning into him.

"I love you, Grace."

Pain pierced her heart, shredding the organ. He loved her, but not enough to marry her. It would have been better for him to never tell her. Now she would carry the truth of his love with her and also face the impossibility of them ever being together.

"And I love you, Sanford."

She managed a tremulous smile. She was on the cusp of breaking. Of bursting into uncontrollable sobs.

This needed to end.

Now.

"But it makes no difference, does it?" She shifted to rise. "If you will excuse me, please."

"Wait." He grasped her hand and scooted to sit beside her.

Shaking her head, Grace refused to meet his eyes. She could bear no more.

"No. There is nothing more to say."

"Please hear me out." Desperation colored his rumbling baritone. "Then, I shall not stop you if you still want to leave."

A surge of anger fortified her.

"Why should I, Sanford? So you can torment me further? Reiterate why I am beneath you? Why I am good enough to bed but not wed?"

Tears leaked from the corners of her eyes.

"I cannot bear any more pain, Sanford. I cannot."

With his thumbs, he brushed away her tears.

"I never meant to hurt you, Grace. I know I did, darling, but I have come to my senses. You made me see what mattered. I have been such a stupid beef-witted fool—until you came into my life and made me understand what was truly important."

He tipped her chin up with his forefinger, forcing her to meet his eyes.

The brown orbs held a promise.

"I spoke the truth when I said I believe we are destined to be together. I want to marry you. Please say it is not too late for us."

What?

Grace's jaw went slack, and she almost put her fingers in her ears to clean them out. Surely, she'd heard wrong.

"What?"

"Marry me, Grace." Sanford pressed a hot kiss to her wrist. "I do not care about what anyone else thinks. I only care about you. Us being together."

Afraid to believe he was serious but desperately wanting it to be so, she searched his earnest features.

"But you have always adhered to society's strictures, Sanford. You must be aware that you will be mocked and ridiculed? Quite possibly shunned and cut, perchance even ostracized."

Laughter echoed outside, and she cast a self-conscious glance toward the window.

Chatting gaily, the Brockmans wandered the tidy garden paths, stopping every now and then to point at a blossom.

"I no longer care about any of that," Sanford said, drawing her attention back to him.

He shook his head and gave a self-deprecating chuckle, his focus shifting to the garden too.

"Have you seen how ridiculously happy my brothers are? How ecstatic Corinna is? Every one of my siblings married people *le beau monde* frowned upon, and I would wager my life, not one of them regrets it one iota."

Grace had only spent time with Ronan and Mercy, but she had never witnessed two people more in love. She longed for that tenderness, that oneness.

"I want what they have, sweetheart." Sanford skimmed his fervent gaze over her face. "I only can if you consent to be my countess."

"I want to say yes." Grace did with every ounce of her being. But what if he changed his mind? "

Are you positive, Sanford? I could not bear it if you had regrets or second thoughts later."

"Never," he vowed so ferociously she blinked up at him.

"I am a man of my word. My honor is paramount to me. I pledge before you and before God that I shall never love another. If you refuse me, I shall respect your decision, but I shall not stop trying to convince you. I shall never take a wife if you will not marry me."

He was serious.

She could see it in the set of his chiseled jaw and the inflexible contours of his face.

He wanted her and no other.

Joy enshrouded Grace. "Then, how can I possibly refuse?"

He whooped and scooped her into his lap and pressed his rough face into her neck.

"Thank God. I was prepared to write poems and sing sonnets. Trust me when I tell you I do not have a voice. My singing incites hounds to howl."

Giggling, Grace squirmed on his lap.

"You are scratching me, Sanford." She scrunched

her nose. "And you do need a bath."

He lifted his head, a boyish grin splitting his face. "I think we should seal our betrothal with a kiss, and then I shall see to my appearance."

"Oh, I quite agree." She entwined her arms around his neck and raised her face to his.

He covered her mouth with his, plundering its depth until Grace's head swam and her breath came in little panting gasps. If his kisses could turn her bones to butter, imagine what their joining would be like?

Persistent rapping on glass made them break apart and glance toward the garden. The entire Brockman family peered in the window, all wearing ridiculous grins.

"Does this mean you are truly betrothed?" Benjamin shouted.

Heart overflowing with happiness, Grace grinned and nodded.

Yes. Yes, she and Sanford were to be married.

"Go away," Sanford growled. "And let me show my bride-to-be how much I adore her."

"Take a bath first," Marissa called before bursting

into giggles and holding her nose.

Her parents ushered her away amid a chorus of laughter.

"Care to join me?" Sanford asked Grace naughtily while waggling his eyebrows.

"Why, Lord Renshaw, you have a sense of humor after all." She leaned back and brushed a shock of hair off his forehead. "What other surprises can I expect?"

"You will have a lifetime to find out, my love."

Epilogue

Pelandale House

June 1829

Drawing little figure eights on his wife's shoulder, Sanford kissed her forehead, then her nose, and finally her mouth.

"Good morning, Lady Renshaw."

Cracking an eye open, Grace yawned and stretched.

"What time is it?" she asked drowsily.

"Time for our children to wake their parents." He raised his head, listening. "Quick, pretend to be asleep. I hear them coming."

Sure enough, the sound of small feet pattering echoed in the corridor.

As they did every day, Sanford and Grace feigned sleep as their three children, Genevieve, Paul, and

Raphael, rushed into their bedchamber. Genevieve had started the tradition as soon as she could walk, and it had continued with every child.

"Wake up, Papa. Wake up, Mama," the children chimed in unison as they clambered onto the oversized bed and bounced up and down. "Wake up. Wake up."

Growling like a bear, Sanford reared up and captured the two eldest in his arms while Grace encircled two-year-old Raphael in hers. Amidst giggles and squirming, Sanford and Grace kissed and tickled their children.

"Mind Mama's tummy," Sanford warned. "You do not want to hurt your little brother or sister."

"It is a girl," Genny said with the confidence of the eldest child. "That is only fair. Two boys and two girls."

Eight months pregnant, Grace would deliver their fourth child next month.

Sanford's and Grace's gazes met above their children's raven heads, and they shared an intimate smile. With both parents possessing black hair, what other color would their offspring have? Genny and Raphy had their mother's indigo eyes, but Paul's were warm tobacco.

After another five minutes of play, their nurses

discreetly knocked on the door.

"We'll see you at breakfast," Grace assured them as the children scrambled off the bed and waved goodbye.

Once they'd gone, Sanford placed his palm atop her distended belly. The baby kicked, and he grinned. "How are you feeling, my love?"

"Like a whale." Grace placed her hand atop his. "I believe this one is the most active yet. I fear our daughter may be disappointed."

Grace had agreed with Sanford's request to live at Pelandale House since the mansion would come to him eventually. Besides, Father and Rachael doted on the children as they did all of their grandchildren.

That, however, did not mean that he and his countess did not find opportunities to spend romantic interludes at Hydeaway House. A wicked grin tipped his mouth upward as he recalled last Wednesday. Strawberries and whipped cream might've been involved.

Propped up on his elbow, his head resting in his hand, Sanford smiled down at Grace.

"Every day I wake up and thank God you hid in my coach that day. I cannot imagine my life without you, darling."

"And every day, I wake up and cannot believe this fairy tale life is truly mine." Grace cupped his face before pressing a kiss to his chin.

He grazed a kiss across her mouth. "And this is our happy ever after, sweetheart."

Look for LADY TEMPTS A ROGUE,

Daughters of Desire (Scandalous Ladies, Book7

Want a FREE first in series Starter Library
from Collette?

Go to: signup.collettecameron.com/TheRegencyRoseGift
to get a five FREE book bundle.

A LADY, A KISS, A CHRISTMAS WISH

Daughters of Desire (Scandalous Ladies), Book One

Sometimes you have to take a few risks on the road to happily ever after…

He dared to defy tradition…

Lord Brandon Morrisette is a born risk-taker. Instead of claiming his place in society, he became a physician to help the less fortunate. So, when he sees a patient mistreating her sweet, bright-eyed companion, Brandon is determined to help bring some holiday cheer into the poor girl's life. It's the least he can do.

But in truth, he'd like to do *much* more for the kind-hearted beauty who so easily captured his attention…and his heart.

She guards a scandalous secret…

Joy Winterborne can't afford to take risks. If anyone found out about her past, she'd lose *everything*. And getting fired from her companion job would deprive her of the only bright spot in her otherwise dreary life—the time she gets to spend with the charming and oh-so-handsome Dr. Morrisette. Of course, nothing can ever come of her attraction to him. He's nobility, and she's *nobody*. But that doesn't stop her silly heart from wanting…*more*.

With a little luck, some mistletoe, and maybe even a Christmas wish, can Brandon convince Joy to take the greatest risk of all—falling in love?

About the Author

USA Today Bestselling author COLLETTE CAMERON® is renowned for her Scottish and Regency historical romance novels featuring daring rogues, scoundrels, and the strong heroines who capture their hearts. Her stories are filled with inspiration and humor, making them the perfect escape for fans of Sweet-to-Spicy Timeless Romances®. Living in Oregon, Collette is a confessed Cadbury chocoholic and dreams of spending part of her time in Scotland. From the rugged highlands to the refined drawing rooms of Regency England, Collette's stories transport you to another time and place, where love and adventure are just a page away.

Thank you for reading EARL OF RENSHAW. Not only is the book part of the *Wicked Earls' Club* series, but it is also part of my *For the Love of an Earl* series and is connected to my *Daughters of Desire (Scandalous Ladies)* series.

While this story is a sweet Regency romance with mild inspirational overtones, I attempted to tastefully introduce romantic elements and sexual tension. The infrequent mild cursing in the story is not only authentic to the era but, let's face it…very few humans are so perfect they never let an expletive slip once in a while.

Enemies to lovers is one of my favorite romance tropes, as are fake betrothals, class differences, and second chances. EARL OF RENSHAW contains elements of all these, plus a little Cinderellaesque and forbidden love.

In modern culture, we do not think it is a big deal for people from different social standings to marry, but during the Regency Era, it was rare. Titles were used to acquire wealth, property, position, and power. Love matches happened occasionally, but marriages of convenience and arranged marriages were the norms. Forced marriages were not unheard of either.

Even today, some elites deem anyone not born in their social class as inferior. Sanford was an utter prig, but Grace brought him up to snuff quite nicely.

If you are interested in reading the stories of some of the secondary characters named in EARL OF RENSHAW, here are their books:

Lord Ronan and Mercy Brockman – NO LADY FOR THE LORD Daughters of Desire (Scandalous Ladies) Book 2

Caspian and Corinna Graystone – A ROGUE WORTH THE RISK, The Honorable Rogues® Book 8 (The Wedding Wager Anthology).

Joy Morrisette – A LADY, A KISS, A CHRISTMAS WISH Daughters of Desire (Scandalous Ladies) Book 1

Check out the other *For the Love of an Earl* books:

EARL OF WAINTHORPE
EARL OF SCARBOROUGH
EARL OF KEYWORTH

To stay abreast of my other books' releases, subscribe to my newsletter, *The Regency Rose* (the link is below), or visit my author world at collettecameron.com.

If you liked Grace and Sanford's story, please consider leaving a review. Reviews really do help authors.

Hugs,

Collette

www.ingramcontent.com/pod-product-compliance
Lightning Source LLC
Chambersburg PA
CBHW071930190726
48293CB00004B/1219

Five to Four